FREE BOOK

Claim your copy of Running The Game when you sign up for my newsletter and cheer on Pen as she vies for a commission in the military aboard ship. In the Humanity Found space opera series

1

"I don't want to go straight through," Lena said, "or wander too far. We want to get home before the winter closes in."

They were bent over the maps again. Now that the decision was made to head to Haven before returning to the farm, there were only a handful of choices.

Anne was hovering at the edge of the group, listening to the discussion. It wasn't ideal to do this in front of her because she was a stranger, but there was no choice. Keeping the location of the farm secret was easier if they focused on this Haven place and Beta. At least the woman had the sense to keep from interrupting or offering her own opinion. She might be part of their journey now, but she had little road experience.

"Chicago is south of a couple of big towns," Scott said. "Gathering intelligence is still the plan, right?"

"Milwaukee, if we go to the coast and down," Luis said. "Or across to Minneapolis, then down."

"Do you know any of these areas?" Astrid asked. "The safest route is better."

"Not since from before," he said. "I vote we head through to Minneapolis. It gives us options."

One of the benefits of being home was not having to make blind decisions that could kill someone. The only difference between the two cities was that one had more opportunity to visit small towns along the way. By heading to Milwaukee, they would pass through a large part of what used to be a national forest. The only thing that probably changed was that there was no national anymore, and way more forest.

Lena let the others talk over the options, trying not to express her frustration at the lack of facts. The fire was dying down, and they had no further use for it. Once they chose a path, they'd ride out. She dumped a jug of water on the embers and reached for the short-handled spade to cover the ashes after checking for any sign something would flare up. Wildfires still happened. They'd pass a few burned out areas on the way as a reminder of how bad a flareup could get.

"Let me help," Anne said. "I know I'm not part of your team officially, but I'm no freeloader. You need to assign me work, Lena."

Work that would have to be double-checked, Lena thought. Anne had given them no reason to trust her, or any to distrust her, to be fair. And if Lena was honest, Anne had as much experience as she had a year ago.

"Just make sure it's out before we leave," Lena said, handing her the shovel. "We don't need to be outrunning a fire."

Anne stared at the wet mess before stirring the ashes with the blade.

Lena walked over to where the horses waited. They were loaded and ready to set out. The two they'd received in

Liberty, Spot and Beau, fit in with the rest without any trouble. She leaned into Bebop's side and smoothed his mane.

"Ready?" Beattie called out. "We've got a long day ahead of us."

They hadn't needed her for the planning stage. Lena was torn between relief that she didn't need to make a choice, and fear that she hadn't noticed a possible threat. She checked to see where Anne was, in case she hadn't heard Beattie. The woman was staring toward the trees.

"Did you see something?" Lena asked as she motioned for Beattie to pay attention.

Anne turned and shook her head. "Just a stag. He's gone, but it's rutting season. Should we be worried?"

Why would a stag be hiding near their camp?

"Not unless you smell of doe in heat," Astrid said, "or competition."

2

Their destination was months away unless they rode hard. Saving a few days wasn't worth the risk of harming one of the horses, so they kept a steady pace, riding around six hours a day. The scenery didn't change much, and they stayed away from any signs of a community at the beginning.

"It's going to get too hot to ride in the middle of the day soon," Luis said. "We should head out earlier in the day tomorrow."

It was probably mid-June, Lena thought. The days were warm, but never too hot. In a week or so, the most important supply would be clean water. Too easy to get dehydrated in the sun. They had plenty of food, and supplementing it with whatever they found fresh was proving simple.

"We have some time," she said. "Let's ease into it. Find shelter early and then get everyone going just after first light?"

"It's still cold in the morning," Astrid said.

"Maybe get up then and have a leisurely breakfast?" Scott said.

"Like waffles and over-easy eggs with a side of bacon?" Lena asked.

"Lots of coffee refills and maybe some juice?" Luis added.

"I always liked a Benedict for special," Anne said. "Smoked Salmon, Hollandaise, capers."

They had plenty to eat, but nothing anyone mentioned was part of the menu. Oatmeal with dried fruit, tea, maybe a bit of cinnamon.

"Stop," Lena said with a groan. "My taste buds are going to be very disappointed."

Beattie and Astrid had taken up their usual places: Astrid in front, Beattie in back. They all rode in close formation unless someone peeled off to scout. So they were alert to danger, but something had changed when they left Liberty. The tense feeling of being watched, or fear for what they'd find ahead, was gone. Most days, they teased each other, or shared stories about the road or the past.

Something about leaving the mountains behind? Lena wondered.

They'd originally left the highways for the forest because it felt too open. Now, she was relishing the freedom of seeing farther than the closest tree. She shrugged her shoulders and straightened her posture. The light was dimming as the sun moved toward the horizon.

"Let's start looking for a camp," she said. It took longer to set up for the night with two more horses. Mostly because eleven animals took up a lot of space.

They ended up in a small industrial center off the side of the road. One of the warehouses was big enough to hold everything and had a picnic area around the back, likely for the employees to enjoy when there were employees and work.

"The office window is broken," Beattie said. "All the glass is gone. We should barricade the door."

Whoever broke the window had cleared out the contents of the warehouse. Or it was gone long before, and the glass was a separate event? The door had been unlocked, so the office was probably just an entrance point to access the inside the first time.

"It opens inward," Tik said. "We can tie the handle to that pipe to hold it closed."

Half an hour later they were gathered at the picnic table, a fire going a few feet away with pots and a kettle heating on the flames.

Astrid pulled the decks of cards and board games from Spot's, the pack horse's bags. "Who's ready to lose to me tonight?"

She'd shown an aptitude for cards so much so that she won almost every game. Not just poker, which was mostly bluffing, but Gin, Crib, Hearts. It was a contest every night to find a new game she might lose.

"I'm cooking," Lena said, "and I'm out of matchsticks I can bet with."

"I can lend you some," Astrid said. "Fair rates."

Lena turned back to the food they'd unpacked for the meal. The chatter at the table faded into the background as she cooked. Jerky softened in boiling water, dried vegetable packages, Ramen noodles with the stock packets. A thin stew, a little too salty but nutritious, and most people didn't worry about blood pressure or cholesterol these days. Work was physical again, so the bad stuff burned off just the same way as the good.

"Where are we setting watch?" Beattie asked. "There are a bunch of places for people to hide."

"Maybe a patrol of the area would be good before the

sun goes completely down," Anne said. "If our fire hasn't attracted scavengers, we should be okay just setting up inside."

"It's going to rain," Luis said. "We won't guard from outside anyway."

"I'll scout out the area," Tik said. "Beattie? Astrid?"

"Yes," Astrid said. "You all go inside. We'll be back soon."

By the time they'd quieted the horses and set up their sleeping bags, the three scouts returned.

"No one out there," Tik said. "Doesn't look like anyone has been here for a while. Likely another deserted area."

"We can't lock the door," Astrid said. "One of us should be there tonight."

"What about the office?" Anne asked.

Lena walked over and tugged at the rope. "No one will be able to move the door."

In the end, they decided on one guard at the front door, facing the camp.

The rain started as they crawled into their sleeping bags. Beattie was on guard for the first shift, Astrid assigned to the second. Tomorrow night, two others would stand guard.

As the sun finally dropped, the warehouse became a void of darkness, and Lena couldn't see as far as the door.

"WAKE UP," Astrid shouted. "They've fucking stolen from us."

Lena bolted up right and wiggled out of her sleeping bag. Astrid was standing by the pile of backpacks and saddlebags. A much smaller pile than she remembered last night.

"The rope," Beattie said. "They cut the rope and just wandered in and took what they wanted."

"How did we miss it?" Anne asked.

"It was too dark," Lena said. "The guards could only see so much, and we all slept like the dead. What's been taken?"

"The horses are all here," Luis called. "Couldn't get them through the window, I guess."

Mellow was moving packs to the side. "Two sacks of food and one of clothes and trade goods. I'm not sure what was in the third bag, maybe more food and some of the medical supplies. It's not great, but it could have been worse."

Their safety margin. And their feeling of safety. Lena didn't voice her thoughts.

"We've gotten by on less and survived," she said. "We'll do an inventory when we stop for a meal. I don't want to be here if the thieves come back. We'll be scavenging again, but we're good at it."

Anne started helping Luis get the horses ready. "If whoever broke in had to steal from us, what kind of scavenging do you think we'll be doing?"

"They could have killed us and taken it all," Beattie said. "We'll be scavenging far from here, don't worry."

3

That night, they camped in an open field, the moon and stars giving enough light for the guards to see anyone approaching. Lena felt exposed, but it was better than another dark building where they could be robbed again.

"I don't like the fact we lost most of the antiseptic stuff," Mellow said as she helped Lena start the fire. "I'll keep an eye out for the ingredients. We should be able to make some if we can find the right herbs. No oil to mix them with. Just water, so no lovely, smooth balm."

"Better than nothing," Lena said. "At least we still have food. We're lucky they didn't destroy what they couldn't take."

It wasn't uncommon to find a location trashed after being scavenged. Some people were unable to get through their anger and fear from the plague deaths. Some were just that kind of asshole.

"We'll find another place," Mellow said. "Maybe a drugstore, or another Costco."

Anne joined them and Mellow moved away. "I'll look for some plants at the stream," she said.

"Take Tik or someone to protect you," Lena said.

"You think we're being followed?" Anne asked. "Maybe I should get a weapon."

Not without a lot more trust.

"We'll be fine," Lena said. "Just don't wander off."

"Maybe when we scavenge," Anne said, "someone could train me?"

"Maybe," Lena said to end the conversation.

"I wonder why they didn't take the cans," Anne said. "Just the dried goods."

"They took the lightest packs. Cans are really heavy if you don't have a horse or a bike."

"Oh. I hadn't thought of that. It means they went through our bags, right?"

"I have no idea. Let's get the pots on the fire. Everyone will be back soon, and hungry."

Anne opened the bag of kitchen supplies. The fire was burning steadily, so Lena used a pair of tongs to place the rack they used to hold multiple pans over the flames.

Luis joined them moments later. "The horses are restless, but I don't see anything. We should patrol the area tonight, not just guard."

"Horses can be skittish," Anne said. "It's probably nothing."

That was a stupid assumption, Lena thought. It's like she'd never traveled before. The road between Beta and Liberty was no safer than any these days. "It's something," she said. "When everyone gets back, most of us can cover the herd." The idea they had enough horses to consider them a herd almost made her laugh.

"Let's boil the water first," Mellow said as she hauled two buckets' worth to the fire. "Tik's filling the horse buckets."

"Something is out there," Astrid said. "Two wolves. We scared them off, but it might not keep them away. Clean the food containers when we're done so we aren't making us smell more delicious."

Luis swore. "No way there's only two wolves. We can eat later." He ran toward the packs where they'd placed their bows and knives.

A horse screamed and the others joined in. The animals tried to scatter, but they were hitched to trees. Lena bent for a couple of throwing knives as she ran. Grey shadows darted from the trees and leaped to snap at the horses.

Spot broke free and tried to escape. A wolf bigger than anything Lena had seen before brought him down.

"Move!" Astrid yelled. A bolt flew past Lena's ear to sink into the chest of the attacking wolf.

Another went by and hit a second wolf in the flank. The fight was over.

Four shapes melted into the trees. Luis and Mellow went to calm the other horses. Astrid and Beattie followed the wolves.

"Tik and I will guard the supplies," Scott said. "Spot needs mercy."

He was too injured to walk, and too heavy for Lena to drag. The wolf had taken a bite out of Spot's leg and he couldn't be saved.

Mellow joined her. "Do you want me to do it?"

Lena shook her head. "The throat, right?"

"He'll be gone in seconds. Luis will come help pull the carcass away."

They had neither the time nor the skills to properly dress the meat. "We'll leave it for the predators," Lena said.

She took a deep breath and looked Spot in the eye. "Thank you for bringing us this far." When she finished, his blood was soaking the ground.

"Damn," Astrid said as she strode up. "The pack is gone. I don't think our bolt did much damage. We should move on, at least a little."

Lena left Astrid and Beattie to move the carcass and went back to the fire. "Pack up and douse the fire. Use water to cool the rack enough," she said. "We'll find another camp."

Luis limped into the circle of light.

"What happened?" Anne asked.

"Mellow will check, but it should be fine. Just hurts like a son of a bitch. River didn't mean to kick."

"I'll need the light to see how bad it is," Mellow said as she approached with the bag of medical supplies. "We don't have anything left for pain, but we still need to know."

"We'll get ready," Astrid said. "Douse the fire when you're done. Anne, come help."

"Drop your pants," Mellow said.

"It's on my calf. I'll pull them up," Luis said.

"I need to see the whole leg," Mellow said. "Don't be shy."

The horseshoe shape was raised, and Lena could see discoloration already on his leg. Mellow prodded the skin around, ignoring Luis's grunts of pain.

"It didn't get to the bone. If it gets more painful or swells up, I need to know. Otherwise, I'll check in the morning." Mellow turned over the packages in her bag. "I'm sorry, those thieves took the last of our aspirin."

"I'll survive. Too bad we don't have any whiskey." Luis pulled up his pants. "I might need some help getting on Junior."

4

Lena shorted the rations to make their supplies last longer. No one went exactly hungry, but no one felt full.

"Better than on the way out," Scott said. "We'll find something soon, and there's still plenty of small game."

"I don't know if that makes me feel better," Anne said. "I had a couple of lean days, too, before I made it to Liberty. There wasn't much left to take when we traveled."

The woman seemed to find a way to be pessimistic about everything, Lena thought. Maybe it was her history on the road, losing her team and having to rely on strangers. Or perhaps she'd always been the kind of person who feared being disappointed. Never reaching for hope because she didn't think anything could be better.

Astrid rode toward them from her scouting trip.

"Maybe they found something?" Mellow said. "She wouldn't come back alone if there was something wrong."

"Maybe she's alone because something went wrong," Anne said.

"She'd be coming faster," Luis said. He shifted in the

saddle and stretched his leg out. The bruise was healing, but riding all day didn't give him a chance to keep from getting stiff.

"We found something," Astrid said as she pulled Raven to a stop. "Not a lot, but some stuff. It's just at the next exit. A Walmart, and another Costco, and a Staples. No one hanging around. This time we checked the roofs, too."

"Staples won't likely hold much for us," Anne said, "unless you think an office chair is something useful."

"There could be notebooks," Mellow said. "One of the packs we lost was our paper. I'd love to start recording our journey again."

"If it's clear, we should look," Lena said. "You never know what gets left behind with sloppy scavenging."

Anne pursed her lips and nudged Beau forward.

In the Staples, Mellow found a couple of packs of plastic-wrapped spiral notebooks under a pile of shattered laptops. Everything else was soaked through when the sprinklers came on to stop a fire that someone had set in the craft aisle.

The Walmart had received the same treatment, as had the Costco.

"We should move on," Anne said. "I don't want to camp here. It's bad enough everyone has disappeared, but to see this? I can't settle."

"This was done not that long ago," Luis said. "The water hasn't evaporated. Not everyone has disappeared."

"There's something in the back," Tik said. "The Walmart, a locked door. Whoever trashed the place couldn't get it open."

"How will we?" Anne said.

"Come look," Tik said. "You can stay with the horses, Anne. We'll be back in a few."

Lena was happy that Anne annoyed Tik, and maybe the others. Not that having an irritating companion was ideal, and she wouldn't abandon the woman, but if it was widespread, she could deal with it. If it was only her, then it seemed too personal.

She handed Anne Bebop's reins and followed Tik.

"You think maybe her original group kicked her out?" he asked. "And the people in Liberty?"

"I'll talk to her," Lena said. "Show me what you found."

Tik led her through the piles of destruction in the aisles. She didn't understand the thought process behind the actions. Anything left behind was useless to the people who released so much rage. Or anyone coming after in need. Perhaps this gang had no one to lead them.

Perhaps they were driven by fury, or simply stoned on the last of the pharmaceuticals.

She stopped at the door. A roll-up metal affair that probably led to the warehouse. If no one had breached it, there could be supplies for years.

"You can see they tried to get in," Tik said, pointing to dents and bends in the metal where someone had tried to pry or smash their way in. "I guess this store had problems with theft well before the plagues."

"They did," she said. "So how do you think we're going to get inside?"

"Brains," he said. "The people who did all the damage gave up when violence didn't work. Astrid and Scott are on the roof looking for a way in. Maybe a skylight or something. Beattie is going through the office and cash desks looking for a key."

"There won't be a key," Lena said. "Card access. See that pad?"

Tik poked at the reader. "I guess it's out of power. Battery?"

"Yes, but you won't find one to replace it," she said. "Technicians would have a way. And the cards are probably deactivated from the fire or the water."

She wondered why it hadn't released the door when it ran out of power. Probably a safety feature. The employees would have a process, or a schedule to replace the batteries. She gave it a shove with her hand to see if it would slide. Not that she expected it to release the door, but because she needed to do something.

"It rises a bit," Tik said. "If we lift the door, maybe we can use something to cut whatever is locking it down."

That won't work, Lena thought. "When they were looking on the roof for spies, did anyone see skylights?"

"That's why they went up," Tik said. "Yes, but not many in the back where we need them."

"If we get through, there's not enough light to let us look around. We'll probably need those wind-up flashlights."

"Did you hear that?" Tik asked. "Something fell inside."

"Did they take ropes?"

"Of course," Tik said. "We have no idea if this will open from the inside."

They waited with their ears pressed to the door. Lena heard banging and a lot of swear words. "Astrid's in there."

No more sounds came from inside for a long time.

"**H**ey!" Astrid yelled from the front of the store. "I found the back door."

It turned out that the roll door was bolted down inside. But thanks to safety issues, a back door opened into a nook. How the raiders had missed it was beyond Lena.

Astrid told Anne to bring the horses around to the side of the building. "Don't want anyone noticing them."

The door was down the side of the loading ramp and sat flush so it would be invisible to a casual look. Scott was holding it open for them. "Grab something to use as a doorstop," he said. "It's a treasure in there."

Inside it was exactly what Lena hoped. The warehouse for the whole store, and it looked like the shelves had been fully stocked before everyone left. There would be back-packs and camping supplies, food, blankets and everything else they needed.

"Check to make sure everything is in good shape," she said. "We need food and some backpacks to replace what was stolen. We need to stock up and go. I don't want to run into the raiders."

Within an hour, the horses were loaded with replacement supplies and a few new items. Cans of Sterno and a camp stove so they didn't need to rely on the fire. Three full bags of dried food and another two of canned. A backpack full of coffee and tea, and another with spices to trade. A handful of knives for hunting or trade, and an insulated cooler with medications and first aid supplies.

"We're better off than before," Anne said. "I've never been so happy to be wrong."

"You know we would have stopped here anyway," Lena said, "even if we weren't robbed. No one passes an opportunity to find supplies."

"Sure, but would we have tried so hard to get into the back?"

Maybe not, Lena admitted to herself.

"Can we remove the lock on that door?" she asked. "If we just close it, all that stuff will just sit there on the shelf."

"Get me the axe," Scott said.

"Let's not wreck ours," Luis said. "I saw some inside. Give me a second."

"Should we leave markers?" Astrid asked. "We can't just prop it open because it will fill with vermin."

Luis limped back carrying a short-handled axe. "We'll take this with us." His first swing sliced the handle off the inside of the door.

"That should do it," Scott said.

An owl hooted. It was broad daylight.

"Raiders," Beattie shouted.

A rock hit the side of the wall.

Astrid shot a bolt into the shrubs, a curse came.

"I can deal with them," she said.

"It's not worth fighting over," Lena said. "Let's get out of here before they decide to rush us. If the raiders are close enough to hit the wall with a rock, they can see the door. And we're not that interesting compared to the contents."

Lena's plan worked. The raiders went for the contents of the warehouse rather than following them. Her nerves were stretched regardless, and she kept looking over her shoulder as they rode.

A thin column of smoke rose from the direction of the Walmart within a half hour. What a waste. On second thought, maybe it was better that survivors were forced to stop relying on the remnants of the old world.

Even if she couldn't bring unity across the country, Lena knew raiders would eventually die off, either turning on their own or being shut down by new communities. The worry was if these roaming gangs found a leader. That was a unity she didn't want.

They rode long into the evening, pushing the horses to put distance between them and the destruction. Far enough that they wouldn't be up through the night watching for an attack. They wanted to feel safe enough to put out the regular watch.

Another night camping in an open field off the side of

the road. Once part of a farm, patches of rye fought for life with grass and weeds, and it seemed to be losing.

Lena picked a site in the middle of the field. A location that gave them clear sight of anyone trying to sneak up on them. The horses were staked nearby, and their packs provided a windbreak for the humans.

It was late enough in the year to avoid freezing temperatures at night so very little needed to be unpacked. Lena was insistent that they have a fast exit. Being able to escape from human or animal predators without losing their precious stores became more important than comfort on the road.

Tik dug and lined a firepit before setting a hearth for their camp stove. The newly acquired solid fuel would keep for when they camped indoors.

"We'll need the fire to see," he said when Anne questioned him. "Low enough to protect our night vision, high enough to show anyone within attacking distance."

Luis returned from his search for water. "I'll fill the collapsible buckets. We don't want the horses out of our sight. Set the rest to boil and use what's left in the waterskins." The last was directed at Anne, who had reached for the spring water.

"Are we opening the cans?" Anne asked Lena. "There aren't many left, and we've got a long road ahead of just jerky and beans."

Did the woman have no road sense?

"Always eat the heavy stuff first," Lena said. Now was the time to talk to Anne about her negativity, but she couldn't think of an opening. "Did you see anything while we were stocking up?" The convenient appearance of the raiders bothered her.

"You think we did something to alert them?" Anne

asked. "I was thinking the same thing. And when we were robbed. It's hard to imagine the guards not noticing."

"We were all tired," Lena said, "and it was dark. People can move silently when they need to."

"I'm just saying, it's weird." Anne started opening cans and pouring the contents into pots.

"That's enough," Lena said. "Save some for morning."

Anne looked at the can in her hand and Lena thought she was going to argue. "I got carried away," Anne said. "I guess I'm really hungry."

"So, did you?" Lena asked. "Notice anything back there?"

"No. But that doesn't mean anything. Astrid and Scott were on the roof, someone could have seen them from a distance. The noise she made when she broke that skylight would have carried. Maybe she should have thought about that."

Astrid would never give them away, Lena thought.

"I guess we'll never know," Lena said. "It could have been a coincidence."

"You send people out in pairs," Anne said. "Because you don't trust them?"

Was this a new tactic to undermine the group, or was it a facet of her pessimism?

"For safety," Lena said. "We've learned that everyone needs cover."

"That makes sense too," Anne said.

Lena couldn't put off the conversation she'd promised Tik she'd have. "Anne, could you tone down the negativity? It's hard enough to travel like this without hearing the worst case every time."

Anne shrugged. "I'm just being practical. It's dangerous to go into everything with blind hope."

Does she think we stumbled our way across the country? Lena set the pots on the camp stove, giving herself time to process her irritation. If Anne didn't trust them to keep her safe, or if she needed to feel completely safe all the time, why did she come with them?

"Can you grab the bowls?" Lena asked. "Everyone will be back soon."

Anne moved away as Lena intended with the words.

She needed time to think through a suspicion. Was Anne the cause of all, or even some of the problems? If so, why would she try to sabotage them? It didn't make sense, which meant Lena was missing information or was paranoid. Both of which could be true.

If Anne was acting against them, she was doing a good job. Attacking morale with her negative comments. Making subtle and not so subtle accusations.

The theft could have been an inside job to slow them down, and there was no proof anyone had broken in other than the cut rope, which would have been difficult to do from the outside so quietly. But for Anne, easy.

The woman was alone while they were in the warehouse grabbing what they could. It would have been a simple job to catch the attention of the raiders.

"Here," Anne said, placing the bowls beside Lena for serving. "Everyone is coming back. It's going to be dark soon."

Lena served a portion of each pot. Stew, canned mushrooms, creamed corn. It would be a tasty dinner. Anne handed out the bowls and waited for the last spoonfuls before taking her own.

"I will try to be more positive," she said quietly. "I guess you know what you're doing."

Lena nodded acknowledgment. And I will watch you closely, she thought. I need to know if I'm paranoid before acting on these suspicions.

7

B eing on the road constantly was more draining than Lena remembered. *In the past, I didn't carry this fear that one of our group was a traitor.*

Watching Anne for signs she was sabotaging the group didn't reveal anything concrete. To her credit, the woman tried to be more positive when she talked. From Lena's perspective, it was less pessimistic rather than positive, but people could only change so much. Anne never mentioned her suspicions again.

The days were warmer, the memory of huddling in the saddle to glean a tiny spark of warmth in the winter had faded weeks ago. Soon, the heat would force them to rest in the middle of the day.

Their road led through farming areas, if not actual farms, now. The forest fell away as they moved closer to the lowlands. Lena preferred to see around her rather than feel crowded by trees.

"I think we should start checking the side roads," Scott said. "The raiders are way behind us. That doesn't mean we're safe. We need to see if there are new threats."

And communities, Lena thought. There must be some people around. The whole country couldn't be empty.

"Astrid and I'll go," Beattie said. "Just keep moving along the road, we'll find you."

"I can come," Anne said. "I feel like I'm kind of freeloading. I need to do something to contribute."

The first time she expressed a need to do something more than camp work.

"Fine," Astrid said. "Stick with us. Don't make any stupid moves. When we tell you to do something, do it without asking questions."

Beattie hid a smile behind a cough. Lena watched to see how Anne reacted. She simply nodded and nudged her horse forward.

While the three scouts rode into the fields, Lena called a halt. "I think the horses need water," she said.

"And you want to talk without Anne around," Scott said.

"I hope I'm not that obvious." Lena dismounted and led Bebop to a small stream that ran parallel to the road.

"You've been watching her like a hawk," Mellow said. "Why haven't you said anything?"

Lena hadn't wanted to poison the rest of the group against the woman. As each day went by after their talk, her suspicion had faded.

"I didn't have anything concrete to go on," Lena said. "She's changed a bit, and I thought I was crazy." She told them about the accusations and suspicions.

"I think you worry about us," Luis said. "She's new and hasn't shared our experiences. We ran into some bad luck, and you wanted a reason for it."

"I suppose," Lena said. "If no one else is worried, I guess I'll back off."

"Never let your guard down completely," Tik said.

"We've had our share of betrayal. I think she's just bad at trusting and reading people, but we don't know her."

"Okay, just try not to let her know we're watching," Lena said. Sharing her worries hadn't made them weaker. She hated being suspicious, but if there was one lesson they'd learned over the whole trip, it was that you can't just trust people.

THE SCOUTS DIDN'T RETURN until Mellow and Lena set up the camp. She didn't worry; Beattie and Astrid could deal with threats, and they would look out for Anne if she needed it. Astrid would bitch about it all night, but they wouldn't leave her behind in a dangerous situation.

"Three small places," Beattie said. "Not interested in visitors, but there's a larger community a half day's ride from here that might be willing to let us stay if we have trade goods or news."

"We should go there," Scott said. "I think we need a break from the road, and it will be nice to have people around."

"Is that something you've done before?" Anne asked. "Just turned up somewhere and stuck around?"

Had the woman forgotten about their stay in Beta? Lena's suspicions spiked again. Granted, she wasn't there when they arrived, but Lena and the others had shared their stories. Not just about Beta, but then thinking back on the other stories, history could be the problem.

"Yes," Mellow said before Lena could reply. "We've had mixed reactions. Is there a reason you don't think we should stay?"

"It's different when you're alone," Anne said. "I guess you know the risks."

Lena let the subject die. Despite all evidence, she found her dream of unity gain some strength. Maybe, like Scott, the idea of meeting new people raised her spirits. The weeks of riding through empty countryside had made her desperate for contact.

They set up for the night, arranged a bag of items for trade and reminisced about the early days of the journey. Whatever emptied the west of people hadn't happened back east. No one talked of the farm, either. Not about the people they'd left behind or the communities around it. Only the original four travelers knew the location.

"I'll take first watch," Scott said. "Who's next?"

"We should have two per shift," Beattie said. "We don't know enough about the people around us."

"I'll share with Scott," Lena said.

The other shifts were filled quickly. Mellow and Tik took second, Astrid and Beattie third. Sharing watch was a chance to have some private time.

Lena leaned against Scott and felt his warmth while she kept her eye on the camp. Nothing unusual happened. Luis was a little closer to the horses than the others. Anne curled up in her sleeping bag and didn't move. She didn't seem worried that they never let her sit watch.

"We'll be back on the farm before you know it," Scott murmured. "Maybe we can find some time to camp out together, just us, before winter pushes us all into the house."

"If it wasn't for the dangers, I'd do this every night," she said. "If it was only you and me, we could enjoy the peace."

"It's all temporary, Lena," he said. "We'll be looking back on this as an adventure soon enough. Tomorrow, maybe you'll find an ally."

"I'd be happy to get information," she said.

Something snapped a twig in the hedgerow. Lena picked

up a stone from the pile they'd gathered and tossed it toward the noise. An animal ran from the sound of it hitting the ground.

"Dog? Something about that size," she said.

"Maybe a deer," Scott said. "We need to hunt soon."

WHEN THEIR SHIFT WAS OVER, Lena fell into a deep dreamless sleep.

Astrid prodded her awake the next dawn. Breakfast was already going, and someone was making coffee from the supply they'd found in the Walmart.

As she rolled out of the cover, Lena resolved to put all her suspicions aside and focus on meeting the new community leader.

"Anne took a walk last night," Astrid said. "Not a bathroom break, she was gone for an hour."

8

Novo Estes. The name of the community they'd approached earlier was small and not part of an old-world town. Their leader, Jack Munson, invited them in without demanding any payment.

There were probably two or three hundred people living together. The streets were unpaved, and the houses looked like they were from an old west tourist town. People nodded as they passed. The stables were clean and only half full.

"We hunt daily," Jack said. "Your horses will be safe here. We built this in the first couple of years after the plagues ended. Started with tents and RVs, then made ourselves more permanent."

Lena fought the urge to relax. Novo Estes looked peaceful and productive. So had Pearl Two and Nicolette's cult, for that matter.

"Do you have any problems?" Beattie asked. "We ran into a bunch of raiders a few weeks back, but after that, the country was empty."

"None around here," Jack said. "Mostly our problems come from weather or hungry bears. Heard a bit about problems north of here, but we're too far from the roads to know what's going on out there."

"Your neighbors were pretty fast in giving us directions," Anne said.

"We have trade agreements around here. Five small communities. We do a bit of specialization. Ours is hunting, some of the others farm, one is on the river. Fish makes a nice change from deer or moose meat."

Jack's mention of the agreements gave Lena hope that he'd be interested in a wider alliance, but they were a long way from the farm, and strong partnerships needed proximity these days. Something pinched in Lena's gut. Was that the problem? So simple that she could have saved a lot heartache by staying home.

She didn't continue the conversation. Standing beside the stables and chatting was not the best way to gather information on anything or share ideas.

"We're not staying long," Lena said. "A couple of days. We're happy to work or help out while we're here."

"Rest up," Jack said. "Your rooms should be ready. We turned the old RVs into a kind of hotel. Not five star, but what is these days? We'll talk around dinner if that's okay. Set up a big barbecue, give you time to meet a bunch more of us."

The RVs were lined up under the shade of a copse of oak trees. Someone had rigged an outdoor shower and a row of outhouses. Jack was wrong; this was what passed for five star when you were used to sleeping bags under the sky.

"We host the market on a rotating basis. Usually have people staying during that time," Jack said. "Settle in. I'll send someone to collect you when dinner's ready. About two hours."

He didn't wait for an answer, and in minutes, they were

alone. Astrid walked through each of the RVs saying it was for safety, but Lena suspected she was looking for the best rooms.

"How much will we unpack?" Anne asked. "I don't like the idea of leaving our stuff out while we party."

They'd managed to carry all the packs from the horses to the RVs to keep an eye on their supplies. Lena agreed with Anne. They'd worked too hard to gather everything. It was stupid to risk them being stolen.

"Just what you'd normally do for a camp," Beattie said. "I'm taking the first shower. We all need one. And maybe there's time for a bit of laundry in the stall, too. Clean clothes will make our trip easier."

The shower was a bucket of water with a screen to make the water spread out when it was tipped. There were three full ones, one on the shower ready to go, and a stack of empty buckets. By the time everyone had cleaned up, and washed out a few outfits, the ground around the shower was mud.

"I HATE THIS," Lena said to Scott as they walked toward the crowd of people at the barbecue.

"Dinner?" he asked.

"No, I love dinner." She laughed. "Maybe it's just me, but I can't trust that this is real. Like that's not moose or venison."

She'd been relieved when keys arrived so they could lock the RVs and not have to set a guard. But after everything that had happened to them recently, she couldn't let go of her fears about being tricked.

"They aren't cannibals," he whispered. "We wouldn't

have been allowed to shower. They'd want to do that themselves. Make sure we were properly clean and marinated."

She jabbed his rib in revenge for the teasing.

"Welcome," Jack said. "Grab a plate and food. I've saved you places near me."

When they were seated, Jack stood and introduced them to the rest of the people sitting at the table. Only fifty of the residents sat at the table with them. Others sat on the ground in what looked like family groups. Others served them, and Lena figured some were working elsewhere. No community could drop all the tasks needed to keep them safe and healthy.

"You must have some good stories," Jack said when he'd finished his short speech. "Been on the road a while by the look of you when you came in."

"Yes," Anne said. "You ever hear of Liberty?"

"Nope. Any reason we should?"

Anne refilled their glasses as she spoke. "North and west of here. Marketplace. Lots of people travel there to trade."

"Not from here," he said.

"We've been on the road about a year and a half," Lena said. "Not all of us. Our group expands and contracts." She wondered why Anne was so open about where they'd come from. "The country is starting to recover in places."

"The country can do what it wants," a man who placed bowls of bread on the table said. "We do good enough here without help."

Lean glanced at Jack to see how he took the man's words. Was he upset someone had put in their opinion?

"For now," Jack said. "Eventually we'll need to go out, but for now we're okay."

The evening passed with stories from the travelers and

the townspeople. Luis shared his experiences from before he'd met them in that parking lot without too much detail.

Jack talked about the early years.

"It sounds bad back west," Jack said as the talk died down. "Gangs? Vast empty spaces? Something is wrong for sure."

"I don't know if it's wrong," Anne said. "We didn't see signs of fighting or anything. Just like the people dropped everything and left."

"Maybe your monks convinced them to join up," Jack said.

Luis had left out the battle with Ambrose's fighters when telling about their wandering evangelists. A good idea, so Jack's people wouldn't view the newcomers as killers, Lena thought.

"We're headed home now," Lena said. "A quick trip down south and then I think we've all had enough of sleeping on the ground."

"We'll stock you up with some travel meat if you have something to trade," Jack said. "Not jerky, but not far off."

While they hadn't discussed her dream of unity, the little comments and responses had sent a clear message that this place wasn't looking for allies beyond their immediate neighbors.

"We have some camping stuff," Anne said. "Knives."

"We'll leave in the morning," Lena said, pushing her empty plate to the center of the table. "That was a feast. It's been a while since we had so much food."

"Sorry you don't want to stay any longer," Jack said. "I'll come by with the meat and look at your trade stuff just after sunrise."

. . .

LUIS SAID he'd spend the night sleeping on the ground near the horses as usual. He'd taken the loss of Spot hard and didn't want another nasty surprise.

Lena set the watch schedule and took the first shift. No way was she going to let down her guard, no matter how pleasant Jack seemed.

"They seem nice," Anne said. "We should all get a good night's sleep."

Lena reminded herself that Anne hadn't seen many communities. Her trip from Beta to Liberty was pretty much straight through. And since then, they'd only seen the bad.

"I'd prefer we keep an eye out," she said. "You told them we have more than we need when you offered to trade. You should know better. Even before the plagues, horrible things could be covered with a nice-looking veneer."

9

Nothing happened in the night. Lena tried to feel positive about that, but the little voice inside said that the community was simply waiting to take them down on the road. Keep the mess away from home.

They were packed and ready to ride, a small bag of trade items on the ground waiting for Jack to come by.

"Maybe we should head out now," Beattie said. "A couple of us."

"Let's give him time," Lena said. "I'd rather not split us up. And we need that meat he promised."

"He's coming," Anne said.

She pointed across the open field where Jack walked toward them carrying a large parcel. He must not be expecting much in the way of trade, Lena thought. Coming alone showed trust; why can't I feel the same?

"This will keep about a week," Jack said as he unrolled the package. The meat inside was dried but still soft. Long strips with patches of fat. "Preserved in salt. You soak it and it will soften more. Don't try eating it raw. Needs to be cooked a while."

Lena thanked him and emptied the trade goods. "Is any of this useful?"

Three of their knives and a bundle of clothes that didn't fit anyone in the group. Things no one needed and would leave room for more valuable items.

"Plenty, thanks. I need a word now we're alone," he said. "I don't like my citizens hearing too much bad about the outside world. Hard to keep them hopeful with some of the shit I hear."

Lena passed the food to Anne to stuff in a saddlebag. "There's some really bad things happening," she said. "Some good, too. I'm sorry if some of our experiences were too much for them to hear."

"That's not it at all," he said. "Good stories are worth it. And the bad stuff is a long way away. You want your group to hear?"

"Secrets aren't healthy when you're traveling for this long," she said.

"Those monks came near us a while back. We lost a few to their message. Sent them somewhere we weren't to know. Like it was a part of the conversion."

"What happened after they left?" Astrid asked. "The ones Lena met didn't take rejection well."

Anne stepped a little closer. She hadn't heard the story of the attack either.

"Yeah, we convinced them to keep moving along," Jack said. "You?"

"We don't talk about it," Scott said, "but they won't bother us again."

Jack checked to make sure no one had followed him. "Thing is, I knew a couple of the people who left pretty well. Expected them to come back after thinking on it for a day or two. No one did."

"Maybe they found comfort," Anne said. "Maybe your reaction was enough to keep them away."

"Maybe," Jack said. "Maybe not. We haven't had anyone come by from that direction in too long. We looked. Hunters are all good trackers. They headed south. Lost their track on the road. Like they knew we'd come looking."

Chicago is in that direction, Lena thought.

"Do you get a lot of travelers stopping?" Astrid asked.

"Not a lot, but enough. In the early days, from all over. People looking for a safe place. Now, not from the south. Don't know if it's because they found homes, or if something is stopping them. Just thought you should hear it from me."

"Why don't your citizens notice?" Anne asked. "Maybe one of them is out there pointing the way west. Discouraging people from coming close."

"No reason to do that," Jack said. "We're big enough, but there's room for more people who don't mind hard work. We got plans for making the town more permanent, so more strong backs are valuable. We don't force people to believe in a bunch of stupid rules."

"No? What about religion?" Anne asked.

"Got some people who pray," Jack said. "Some to Allah, some to God or gods, some to the trees and seasons. We don't mind as long as they let others believe or not as they want."

Lena put her hand on Anne's arm. "Go mount up," she said.

When they were alone again, Lena thanked Jack for the warning. "Who knows what's real," she said. "I need to know in case it's a danger to my home. Sorry about Anne, she's new to the road, I think."

"People are allowed to ask questions," Jack said. "We've had strong opinions before. Some move on, some smooth out. Since no one can hear us, would you tell me what happened when you told the monks no?"

This man was trying to protect his people. Lena glanced over to make sure Anne wouldn't hear her answer. "They have soldiers," she whispered. "We killed a few who attacked us. You should be looking for that. How long ago did you run them off?"

"A week. They were headed west, so you won't run into them."

"The soldiers come a few days after," she said. "They don't wear bells, and they are good with swords."

He picked up his payment and thanked her. "I guess we need to set patrols for a while."

10

"What did he say?" Anne asked as soon as the community was behind them.

"He wanted it to be private," Astrid said. "Lena will tell us when she's ready."

Anne stiffened. Something about the question hit Lena as more than simple curiosity.

Astrid's reaction was typical, so why did it make Anne uncomfortable? It seemed the girl always needed someone to be the other, apart from the group. Lena wouldn't interfere this time. Anne was just with them for the ride. She was going back to Beta, not the farm. She could fend for herself with a teenager. If she couldn't, it was her problem. Lena reminded herself not to let Astrid's attitude infect her. Anne was doing her best to be positive after their talk.

"Just rumors about where we're going," she said. "I'm not sure how valid it is. Living in a closed community off the grid can make you insular."

"It was a long conversation for just that," Anne said. "But I'm sure you're right. Our news seemed to be completely new to them."

"He wasn't the most direct person we met," Scott said. "I'm sure he meant well."

Anne looked like she was going to comment further but changed her mind. "How far do you think we'll get today?"

It's a couple of weeks to Minneapolis, Lena thought, if we continued at this pace. Her appetite for stopping in communities on the way was gone. Jack's words didn't discourage Lena; it made finding the truth more urgent. If something or someone was discouraging people from traveling this way, she needed to know.

"Let's go until it's almost dark," she said. "We should probably speed up for a while. Get closer to Chicago while the weather is still mild. I seem to remember summer is hot and humid there."

"Minneapolis in a week?" Astrid asked. "Then Chicago? Or have the plans changed?"

"Plans are the same," Lena said. "I don't see any reason to hang around."

They rode with a short break for the horses for close to ten hours. When it came time to look for a camp, the choices were an open field or another open field. Two rest areas were destroyed, and the few gas stations had been burned out.

"This one is better," Beattie said as they came to a stop in the one that appeared to have produced nothing more than a crop of rocks. "I can hear water, there's no sign of recent occupation, and we can see far enough to defend against anyone coming close."

Lena could see her own fatigue reflected on the faces around her. "I guess we've been spoiled. Let's set up and have some of the meat Jack gave us."

. . .

IT TOOK no time at all to circle the horses and set up a camp to the side. Packs were laid on the ground to mark the line between horse and human space. The ground was so rocky they didn't need to dig a pit for the fire.

The sound of water came from a fast-running stream where Luis and Mellow filled the empty bottles and buckets for boiling just as the sun fell. The fire and the full moon gave just enough light to make them feel comfortable, but not enough for anyone to be safe wandering away.

"The food is good," Tik said. "They know how to process meat for the road."

"I thought it was weird," Anne said. "No one from there goes more than a couple of hours away. Why would they need travel food?"

She'd picked up on something Lena had missed. "Maybe they're planning a trip?"

"Winter," Beattie said. "He didn't call it travel food, right? They need meat through the winter, more calories because it's cold out."

"He seemed a bit defensive when I asked him about religion," Anne said.

She wasn't willing to let the topic go. What had Jack done to earn him this level of suspicion? "I didn't think so," Lena said. "I didn't realize you were a believer."

Anne tossed a small branch onto the fire, sending up a bloom of sparks. "I have an open mind," she said when the fire settled. "Do you think he was telling the truth about all kinds of religions in his community?"

"Why would he lie?" Mellow asked.

"Why do you care?" Astrid butted in before Anne could answer. "We weren't planning to stay. His community; his business."

"Just before, that mostly wasn't true. You were all kids so maybe you don't remember."

Astrid was the only one of the group who might not know what the world was like before. The rest were kids, but not that young.

Lena decided not to get involved. No one in the group needed help to defend their convictions, and Anne was an adult. If she hadn't learned how to get along with people by now, she never would. Watching gave Lena a new perspective on the woman. Would it be better to encourage her to stay in the next community? Or urge her to head back to Beta alone?

The thought of abandoning her when she clearly didn't have the skills to make it was enough to drain the taste from the last bites in Lena's bowl.

"We learned about the world before," Mellow said. "You mean all the wars? Religion was just the excuse. Greed and ego were behind them all."

Anne started collecting the empty bowls. "I guess. But like I said, I like to keep an open mind."

"I'll get some boiled water to wash those," Luis said. "I'm sleeping with the horses again unless you need me to sit watch."

"Why don't you let me guard?" Anne said. "Don't you trust me?"

"No," Astrid said. "Where did you go the other night?"

"I don't know what you are talking about," Anne snapped.

"You left for an hour," Astrid said. "Why?"

Anne shrugged. "I don't remember. You must be mistaken."

Astrid blazed with fury. She reached for the knife she kept in a belt sheath.

Beattie stood and touched Astrid's hand. "Not now," she whispered.

Lena turned her attention to Anne. She'd lied, but was it a threat to the group, or was she embarrassed about something?

"I don't like being accused," Anne said through gritted teeth.

"What are you going to do about it?" Beattie asked. "You can always walk away."

"Stop," Lena said loud enough to cut through to Astrid. "We're tired, and that means we're likely to say something we regret. Let's try to get a night's sleep." She sent Astrid a look that she hoped would be interpreted as 'I believe you but not now,' and regretted not coming up with some kind of sign language in the last eighteen months.

Before Astrid could back down or escalate, Anne stood. "Wait. Do you mean the night before we met Jack?"

"Yes, or have you disappeared more than once?"

Beattie patted Astrid's hand and murmured something in her ear.

"I got lost," Anne said. "I went for a call of nature and I got turned around. It took me a long time to find my way back. I was really hoping no one noticed. Are you happy now you've embarrassed me in front of everyone?"

"Don't do it again," Astrid hissed before sitting.

"In answer to your question, Anne," Beattie said, "we can't afford to change the routine. Enjoy getting a full night's sleep. Sitting and watching the dark fields isn't fun. If you really want to try, sit up with someone."

"You can work with me," Lena said. "First shift is easier." *And I can keep an eye on you.*

"If you don't trust me, then I'll take the sleep," Anne

said. "I just wanted to contribute. I can wash dishes and boil water to do that."

11

The days were hotter now, and they'd moved from the side roads to the highway in search of speed. There was no shade, and few places to rest without taking a long ride from an off ramp, making the journey even longer. The view from the road was monotonous, and the amount of vandalism of the various stores they could see set a pall of depression over the group.

"We're only few miles from the turnoff," Scott said. He held the map folded to their location. No one wanted to dismount while they stopped to make a decision about the city. "We can keep going and rest in the outskirts of Minneapolis. Or rest now and go in tomorrow?"

"There's still plenty of light," Astrid said. "My vote is we have a quick break and then decide when we can think better."

Lena took off the hat she'd found in a store two days ago and fanned her face. The couple of miles would be draining in the heat, but getting to the city today felt right. No matter what they found, there would be shelter close by. Even if the city was overrun with gangs, the outskirts would offer someplace to stop. She leaned into Bebop's neck. He was hot. "Will the horses be okay if we keep going?"

Luis patted Junior's side. "No speed, and they'll need water, but we should be okay."

"Water now?" Anne asked. "We'll need to find some."

"Behind that windbreak," Scott said. "I can see a stream. Someone can climb down the berm and make a few trips."

Without traffic, the highway was much more versatile than before. Often a hop over some concrete barriers let them scout a strip mall. The horses were restricted much like cars were in the cities, but on foot, only the height of an overpass got in the way.

"I'll go," Anne said. "A few buckets of water won't be a problem."

"I'll come," Astrid said. "Who knows what might be hiding there."

"We haven't seen people for two days," Anne said. "I can handle it."

The suspicion about Anne's intentions hadn't completely gone away. Lena found herself reading into everything the woman said or did. Why didn't she want help? Just because it was Astrid who was constantly bickering with her? Or something sinister, like she wanted to slip something into the buckets to slow them down?

"Animals, not humans," Beattie said. "Water means all kinds of danger."

"A few deer won't hurt me," Anne said as she grabbed the waterproof bags.

"If they had a zoo, it won't be deer," Tik said. "Are you going to argue for much longer?"

Anne glanced over to the row of trees hiding the stream that now she was on the ground. Lena thought she was actually going to continue to fight Astrid, but then her body relaxed and she nodded. "I didn't think of that. Fine."

Everyone dismounted and joined Scott at the map. "Is there a zoo?" Lena asked. "Or was that just a tactic to shut her up?"

Scott opened the map up and pointed. "Not that far away. Maybe no lions or tigers, but who knows?"

"She's a pain," Mellow said. "I wish we hadn't brought her along."

"We can't send her on her way," Beattie said. "She's barely equipped for traveling with us, let alone by herself."

"Maybe she feels the same," Luis said. "She's not comfortable relying on us, so it comes out when she talks. It's not like she's avoiding work."

"She's coming back," Tik said.

Lena took one of the waterskins in the pack with sterilized water and passed it around. Watching the horses slurp out of their own bags made her own thirst worse. "Are we in good enough shape to make a decision?"

"Are you ever?" Anne asked. "I mean, from what you say, mostly it's luck whether you see what's going on or not."

Thinking back, Lena agreed. Too many times, they'd thought a place was reasonably safe and were surprised when something went wrong. On this leg of the trip, they'd almost been attacked by raiders, lost a horse, and had their supplies stolen. If Minneapolis was like Pearl Two, would they see it no matter how long they observed? If it was like Seattle, overrun with animals, would it be safe?

"It won't get better," Scott said. "I say we go look. Cities like this have lots of suburbs. We won't be stumbling into a city center where we can be trapped."

How much had things changed since Scott was traveling

alone? Between them, he and Luis had seen a huge part of the country, but Scott's experience was five years old.

"You want to vote?" Anne asked. "Or should Lena decide like usual?"

Why did that make her uncomfortable? The group rarely disagreed, so voting didn't happen, but Lena thought everyone had a voice.

"Anyone want to rest overnight?" Mellow asked. When no one said anything, she turned to Anne. "I guess we go on."

THE OUTSKIRTS of Minneapolis were deserted and looked like they'd been that way for years. Most of the buildings were covered in what would have been called weeds before.

Lena rode Bebop with her crossbow in one hand, a bolt ready to fire if needed. If anyone was using the area for farming, there was no sign, but her shoulders itched with the familiar feeling of being watched.

"A good area for an ambush," Anne said as she pulled up beside Lena. "Should we just get back on the highway?"

"Are you in such a hurry to get to this Haven place?" Lena asked. "It might be different from the rumors. Things change quickly these days."

"I'm more interested in getting out of here alive," Anne said. "This is a waste of time. And we'll need to camp soon. Are you planning to do that in one of the houses? Hoping there's a room inside we can use?"

The woman seemed unable to keep her pessimism under control, or at least inside. Lena swore they'd leave her in the first place she'd be reasonably safe. It was bad enough walking into what could be a trap or a wasteland without her harping on the dangers.

"We need to see what's happening," Lena said. "We can't leave this at our back without a good idea we're safe. And if no one has scavenged, we might find some supplies."

"Are we short again?" Anne asked. "I thought we had enough to get us through the next couple of weeks."

Tik rode up from behind them. "When you travel, having more supplies than you need is important," he said. "And it's not a good idea to proclaim to the world that we have food. You might not feel it, but we're being watched. Not sure if it's a human or a different kind of predator. So, keep alert and keep your mouth shut."

Tik wasn't usually that blunt. Lena wished she'd been more clear with Anne, but maybe tonight when they camped. A lesson on survival might be the way to get through to her.

"I think we move out. Head back to the road as soon as we see what's going on in the city," Lena said loud enough for whoever was watching to hear.

12

The city was in better shape than the suburbs, but only because fewer people had gardens that could run wild. The feeling of being watched faded as soon as they entered the city proper. Perhaps only because they could see less of their surroundings.

"We could camp in one of the empty buildings," Mellow said. "Easy to defend, and we'll have a chance to scout out any scavenging opportunities."

"I thought we were going back to the road," Anne said.

"It's a risk," Scott said. "We can head back to an on ramp, but we won't get far before dark."

"A building is easier to defend," Beattie said. "Open road isn't."

Lena gave Anne a look that cut off her response. Their safety was in Astrid and Beattie's hands. Everyone could fight if needed, but only those two had the right training to know the risks.

"Which one?" she asked. "There are three buildings we can pick."

"You stay here," Astrid said, dismounting. "They all look

abandoned, but let us go first. We'll find a room where we can't be trapped, and we can defend."

Tik handed his reins to Mellow and joined Beattie and Astrid on the pavement. Luis took control of Raven and Strider.

"Circle up and keep watch," Astrid said before they slipped into the first building.

Lena directed the group into a defensive circle and held up her crossbow. "I hate these abandoned cities," she said. "They never feel completely empty. Like the ghosts of everyone who died here are watching."

"Someone was here recently enough to get rid of the bodies," Mellow said. "I wonder why they left."

"It's hard to keep a community alive without farms," Luis said. "It doesn't have the feel of the coast. Like it hasn't been abandoned long. No wild animals in the streets. The roads have been cleared."

Mellow was right. There had been a community here not that long ago. Lena glanced around her. Abandoned cars were lined on the sidewalks, and now that she had time to look closely, it was as though someone had set it up like a maze. If anyone followed the cleared paths, they would be herded somewhere. Likely not somewhere welcoming.

"The second building is clear," Astrid said.

She'd approached without Lena noticing. Had she been so lost in thought that they'd been open to attack? No. The girl was very talented at hiding her movements.

"Beattie and Tik are clearing a space for the horses," Astrid said. "Follow me."

She mounted Raven and led them through the closest intersection to the entrance to a Target. The racks were bare, so they wouldn't be able to replenish their supplies. It did give them space to camp and stable the horses. In fact, there was evidence that someone had done the same not that long ago. Was that reassuring or unnerving? Evidence of travelers after so many deserted places was eerie.

"I'm scouting," Beattie said. "It's not smart to stick around without knowing what's nearby."

When Astrid stepped forward to join her, Beattie shook her head. "Stay with them. I'll be fast and quiet. If someone is watching and they see me leave, it might make them bold enough to attack."

Astrid kissed her. "Don't get killed." Her version of 'I love you'.

"Is Luis going to stick with the horses?" Anne asked. "I mean, I could help with that."

"Help me arrange something for dinner," Lena said. She was going to keep an eye on Anne until they could part company. Letting her take charge of anything was a risk. Of all the people who'd joined the group, Anne was the one who worried her most.

Luis had gained their trust by helping them find their route. Astrid was rescued and cleared Luis' name of all the charges trumped up by the leaders of Virtue. Beattie never gave her a moment's worry. Even Siren proved himself trustworthy in a few days.

Anne didn't do anything in particular, but she was always finding the negative, and her comments carried a tone that didn't sit well. Like the way she said Luis' name. Like he was planning something nefarious.

Anne pulled items from the food pack and placed them on a tarp. "Okay. I just thought switching out was a good idea. No one should get too comfortable, right?"

Comfort wasn't possible on the road, Lena thought. Not just physical, but at every level. There was a threat in every cluster of buildings. Illness still lurked in the form of food poisoning, and just plain common sickness. Injury happened to the most careful. Beattie had been out of commission for a month with a simple scratch.

"Let me worry about that," Lena said. "We've all been together a long time. Done a lot to defend ourselves."

"I guess. But Luis never talks about before," Anne said. "None of you do much, but he never tells anyone what he did before the plagues."

Dwelling on the past wasn't healthy. Either you mourned what you lost because there weren't things like GPS, or grieved who you lost to the diseases — or both. "I didn't realize people shared their stories. What did you do?"

"Marketing," Anne said. She was repacking the supplies they wouldn't need. "No call for getting eyes on a product these days. You were a teacher?"

"I was."

"The others are too young to have much of a life in the old world," Anne said.

What would she think about Tik's history with gangs? Lena took the food Anne handed her and started preparing dinner. "I guess unless a past comes with a skill, it's not my business. Even then, no one is obligated to share."

Anne grunted acknowledgment and didn't keep the subject going.

13

"I saw nothing dangerous," Beattie said when she rejoined them.

"Does that mean we can stay here for a couple of days?" Anne asked.

Beattie grabbed a mug of water and the bowl of soup Lena kept warm for her.

"No. It means if there is something dangerous out there, I didn't see it." She drank half the mugful before she continued. "There's some hint of recent occupation a few blocks away, but nothing permanent. It's odd. That's all. Did someone check the roof?"

"I'll go now," Astrid said. "We were busy settling in. I should have done it right away."

Anne's behavior was starting to disrupt their usual caution. After helping Lena set up the meal, she'd gone to talk to Luis and Astrid. She seemed to think being inside the building meant that they didn't need to use care.

"We're heading out tomorrow," she said. "Every time we stay somewhere for a few days, we risk traveling home in the winter."

"It's only early summer," Anne said. "I think it makes sense to arrive in Chicago rested."

"We have more experience with delays," Scott said. "Time slips by without you realizing. You can stay if you like. No one is forcing you to continue with us."

Lena kept her eyes on the knitting project she'd brought out after the meal. If Scott was reminding Anne she wasn't tied to them, she was annoying everyone.

"I could," Anne said. "Chicago isn't that far to travel alone."

If she was expecting anyone to talk her out of it, Anne was disappointed. Lena rolled the yarn around her project and tucked it back in the pack. "We should remember to call it Haven," she said. "It won't be Chicago, not the old one, anyway, and the inhabitants might be offended by using the old name."

Anne shrugged as if the lack of support didn't matter to her. "I guess they wouldn't have changed it if they wanted to use Chicago."

Astrid walked back through the door with company. "Yeah, so there are people here."

The woman with her was older than Lena, gray curly hair floated loose over her shoulders. She wore an army camo tank and pants. No weapons, and a smile on her face. Lena knew better than to believe her appearance of friendly welcome.

"I'm Alia," the woman said. "Welcome to Minneapolis. We're a small community, but we can offer you a place to rest and share stories."

Lena watched Astrid as she heard Alia talk. There was nothing on the girl's face to indicate danger. She turned when she heard Beattie rise and then glanced around for the rest of the group. Anne was walking toward the horses.

Luis watched her. Scott stood next to Beattie, ready to defend them. Mellow guarded their packs and Tik stood with her. There were no back doors to let an armed group surround them.

"We are passing through," Lena said. She walked over to shake Alia's hand. "If your community is close, we'd be happy to talk."

"Your scout came close to us," Alia said. "We have our own who saw you arrive. We mean no harm. There are reasons we need to stay vigilant."

"Completely understandable. Is there a place for our horses?"

"We set up stables in a park. Yours will be safe with our own herd. And sleeping in a couple of the empty apartments we maintain will be far more comfortable than in here."

14

The stables in the park were spacious and well managed. The manure was piled at the back with a man turning it over to compost. The feed was kept in bins, and a long water trough was available to all the horses. If the rest of the community was as well organized, Lena could see why the leaders had spies keeping watch for threats.

"They'll be safe," Alia said. "If you want to leave someone to watch over them, no one will mind. Especially if they're willing to help with the chores."

Luis leaned on the fence that kept the animals from wandering. "I'll drop by to check them before we sleep," he said. "What's the cost of stabling?"

"For one night, just some stories," Alia said. "Entertainment is pretty rare these days."

An hour later, Lena sat with her companions at a long table in what had been a high school gym. Wine flowed as well as beer, and iced tea for those not imbibing. Lena had opted for the tea after catching a hint of the wine aroma. Raw, and needing a few years in a barrel before it was really drinkable. But alcohol was a good way to cheer people up, even if it didn't taste great.

"If you don't mind, Cici will make notes. We can repeat your stories for years to come if she has a record." Alia pointed to a young black woman with a shaved head and startlingly green eyes. "She's our archivist, I guess that's the closest title. Instead of inundating you with everyone's questions, we'll turn this into a bunch of news bulletins."

"No problem." Lena had already agreed with the others in the group that they wouldn't share anything personal beyond vague background. "I might steal that idea for home. It might be the only way we can keep a history of the time before."

Alia poured another round of drinks and then suggested they start. "Why are you on the road?"

Lena let Scott talk about their adventures on the trip out. Anne provided a little detail about Beta, not as much as Lena expected, but it wasn't her place to add details.

"The northwest is pretty empty," Luis said. "Most of the people live on the coast as far as we could tell. That gang is going to be busy defending themselves for a while, but you should keep an eye out."

"We've seen nothing like that around here," Alia said. "Not that everything is perfect. We're still humans, after all."

Lena took a sip of her tea. The evening was getting late, and Alia had been careful to keep eliciting stories from the travelers. She couldn't wait until morning to learn about the area around the city. If Alia didn't start sharing soon, Lena would find a way to turn the topic around. She was determined to be on the road early.

"So, you haven't been successful," Alia said, "tying the country together again?"

"It's feeling less and less likely the more we travel," Lena said.

"We're too busy staying safe right now, but I can see the benefits in the future. We don't need everything back from before, but reliable communication and food supplies would be good. And a way to travel without fear of kidnapping, theft, or death is probably the first step."

The woman had grasped the challenges fast. "You've had the same idea?" Lena asked.

"Not the same, but close," Alia said. "Give us five years or so and we'll be knocking at your door to sign papers. But you need intelligence for around here, right?"

"We're headed for Haven," Anne said. "All we have are some rumors from way north of here."

"Yeah, Haven," Alia said.

Cici looked up from her notes and grimaced. "Big cities scare me," she said. "Too many people trying to run things. Just like before. I figure the plagues were unleashed because someone didn't like a decision someone else made. Big cities probably still have that problem. Just not the technology to do too much damage."

The theories about the plagues were all over the place. Lena believed that none of them were the full story. That each had a sliver of truth. That the mutated childhood diseases came from a lab, that too many people hadn't kept up vaccinations. That it was too late by the time anyone knew the truth.

"I guess it doesn't really matter," she said. "Whatever caused the plagues to take so many lives is irrelevant to surviving these days."

"Until we get a bigger population," Cici said, "and more ability to kill each other."

"Stop being so jaded, Cici," Alia said. "I figure we'll be

long dead when we have to worry about that again. So, local news."

Lena glanced at the others in her group. Most were, like her, drinking tea. Tik and Beattie had beer in their mugs but had refused refills. They were all tired but perked up at Alia's announcement.

"Cici?" Alia said. "It's your job."

The young woman sat straight and started speaking. She sounded like a news anchor.

"Reports of raiders have increased in the last few weeks. These seem to be desperate people who are not willing to join in a community and abide by our rules. Six cattle and two horses were stolen. A family defending their home encountered weak resistance, but the criminals managed to effect an escape. The roads are safe for travel as long as no one ventures out alone."

"Good to know," Scott said. "We should be okay. What about Haven?"

Alia dismissed Cici and the two other citizens who'd stayed to hear the stories. When they were alone, she poured another beer for herself then looked at the people sitting around the table.

"To be honest, I only have guesses and rumors. The raiders might not be what Cici reported. I've heard that some of the raids weren't reported officially. The raiders are organized and could be recruiting. I think they are coming from old Chicago."

"What makes you think that?" Astrid asked.

"There's a troubling element of psychological pressure. Some effort to convert people to report on our actions. We sent a scout party to this Haven and they said it looked real. That no one was being forced to do anything beyond the usual participation in running the place, but the inhabitants avoided some conversations. Seemed scared of being overheard."

"A bit of discipline is normal," Anne said. "How long were your scouts there? Maybe they didn't stay long enough to make connections."

"A week," Alia said. "They had enough time to get real information. And, this might be coincidence, but the raids ramped up just after the scouts returned."

"Coincidences happen," Anne said. "I think I'll turn in. Anyone coming?"

Lena had heard enough. They were still operating on unconfirmed rumors, but they were going to Haven with their eyes open and a weapon to hand.

Alia gave Lena directions to the three communities between Minneapolis and Haven. "They might have more information for you," she said. "Just don't expect much from them. The land is productive, but they ignore all attempts to help get more out of it than a minimum. I've written the leaders' names down for you. That might have changed, but maybe not."

As they rode toward the first, Lena wondered why anyone would let land go to waste. "I don't want to spend a lot of time visiting," she said to the others over their midday break. "Unless we have a solid reason to go off on a side trip, we should stick with the two that are basically on the way."

"Why do you think these little places will have news?" Anne asked. She stroked Beau's neck and held out her hand with an apple in the palm. The horse took the fruit and stepped back to chew it.

"They are closer," Beattie said. "It's hard to imagine they don't know more. The third one is only a day or two from Haven."

Lena let the others talk. She had her own conflict to

work out. Anne had raised a good point. Was it a worry that this Haven seemed to hide its truth so well? Or should she be happy they didn't have a bad reputation? Going to two of the settlements would only add a day to their journey, maybe a little more if they hung around to exchange stories.

From what little Alia told her, the farms were not much bigger than a few families. Barely enough to work the land. That might explain why they didn't want advice on increasing yield. It wasn't unusual for people to worry that if they have more than they need, strangers would decide to take it. Look at what happened with Newton Cole at the farm.

The conversation ebbed and flowed around her in the heat of the day. She was so deep in her thoughts the words simply blended with the buzz of insects.

Traveling through the day in early July brought its own discomfort. Sure, rain and snow were awful, but mosquito bites and the unrelenting heat drained her more than the cold. Next year, if nothing went off track, they would be able to get out of the worst of it at home. Cold water from the well or iced tea was more refreshing than tepid water carrying the taste of the container. Even if the tea was more like an herbal remedy than the pre-plague variety.

"Lena?" Scott's voice broke through her thoughts.

"Sorry, I was miles away," she said.

"We're ready to head out," he said. "Want to ride at the rear with me?"

Dropping back was the only real way to have a private conversation as they rode. Something was on his mind, and she didn't think it was reminiscing about the farm.

When the horses were moving again, Lena slowed Bebop and let the group gain some ground. No one would mind, because guarding the rear was better from a distance.

"So, what did I miss?" she asked when they were far enough back to have a measure of privacy.

"Not much. The usual bickering. I don't remember it ever being this bad, even when Astrid and Siren were at it."

Anne again. There wasn't anything they could do about her yet. Or more accurately, anything Lena would allow. From what Alia said, it was unlikely either of the two farms would take her in. Haven was their best choice to part ways. Find her someone who would escort her home to Beta.

"It will end eventually," she said. "I don't know why she sticks with us since she doesn't agree with any of our decisions. You think that's why Da Vinci sent her out?"

Scott laughed. "Depends on who he sent with her when she started out. He's more likely to encourage someone so difficult to move on than send them on a scouting mission."

And they only had Anne's word for it. It was just as likely that Da Vinci had suggested she leave than assign her a critical role. "Maybe she wasn't like this at Beta?"

"She's really good at being an irritant, but maybe she was able to hide her nature," Scott said. "That's not what I wanted to talk about."

"Okay." Lena braced herself. If she'd missed something important, it wasn't just a problem.

"I don't like the way Haven is hiding itself. No. That's not right. They aren't hiding. But no one nearby has any idea of their... I guess intentions is the closest word."

So, she hadn't missed anything. "If the farms don't have anything, do you think we turn around and head home? I guess take Anne to Beta and then head for the farm?"

"Let's talk about it after this visit," Scott said. "It would be good if Anne wasn't there when we do it."

The woman had offered to sit with the horses, maybe it was time to give her that duty for the night.

16

The first farm was run by a family named Stevenson. The plagues came just as the bank was foreclosing. The first time Lena heard of anyone benefiting. The visit lasted less than an hour even though Lena and Mellow were the only ones who approached to avoid being seen as a threat. The others stayed on the entrance to the main road. Far enough away that no one would recognize who sat on the horses, close enough that it was clear they were more than two women traveling without company.

"That Haven place don't bother us because we keep to our own," the patriarch told Lena. The man was in his sixties and clearly used to getting his own way.

"Thanks, I appreciate it's safer to keep stronger neighbors at arm's length," Lena said. "We'll be on our way."

"Don't you be telling them you stopped here," he said. "They got spies all over. Looking for any reason to take over."

He walked away leaving the two women wondering if he

was warning them, or just paranoid that someone might take his farm again.

THEIR SECOND STOP the next day was a little more worthwhile. Three families working diverse fields. Well enough off to invite them to share the midday meal.

"We're just passing," Lena said. "Thanks for the invitation, but we need to make up some distance today."

"We do some trading with the folks at Haven," Mike said. He'd walked out to meet them at the gate to the farm. "Hard bargainers, but who can blame them? We get help with the harvest and planting, they get a share of the produce. Never had a problem with them."

He scanned the group as he talked, his eyes never settling on any individual, but he was definitely more cautious than his words suggested.

"Any problems on the road?" Tik asked.

"A few people coming and going," Mike said. "Haven recruits, and people go out exploring. No bandits, if that's what you mean. Having armed peacekeepers nearby tends to discourage the rough kind."

"They keep the road clear?" Lena asked. There could be some good ideas on creating a patrol force from whoever managed it in Haven.

"More with their presence than any purposeful actions," Mike said. "Never heard of violence, but they got fighters. Maybe a little more of that kind than explorers. I don't ask questions."

So, more vague references that leave everything open to her own interpretation. Lena thanked the man and led the group to the road.

17

"I don't want to go in without some kind of intelligence," Beattie said. "There must be a spot we can use to observe."

"I could go in and do a bit of scouting," Astrid said. "A day, then I can report in."

"We aren't getting separated," Lena said. "I know we don't have anything concrete, but it would be a shame to make a stupid mistake just as we're about to head home."

They were camped a couple of hours' ride from Haven. Earlier they'd ridden closer, but turned back when it was obvious they wouldn't be able to get a spy nest set up. Lena had a few ideas about their next steps but wanted to hear everyone's ideas first.

"Look, we should just go in and see what's up," Anne said. "If there was a problem, we would have heard from someone, right? And how are they going to stop us from leaving? The place is open to the land and lake. No city wall, no fences."

"We've learned a few things," Luis said. "The biggest one is to know what you are getting into. There are places without walls where you can get stuck, or killed. You can go in if you like, we'll be smarter about it."

Anne twisted her lips in an effort to keep from arguing. Lena waited to see if she would be able to control her impulse. They'd had a few conversations about her attitude toward Luis, and it seemed to be working — not changing her attitude but keeping it from causing trouble.

"What if we snuck into one of the abandoned skyscrapers?" Scott asked. "On the edge, at night, we could get high enough to see into the city."

Still risky and again would separate them because it would be impossible to keep the entire group stealthy enough. "Any other ideas?"

"You could just go home," Anne said. "If you're this cautious, you probably won't learn anything worth knowing."

"We need to know," Astrid said. "There are two possibilities. This place is a good partner in building Lena's dream, or they are a dangerous enemy. Either way, they are too close to home to ignore."

"Not that close," Anne said, "and there's way more than two possibilities. Haven could just be a good place that doesn't want to get involved. Or they aren't ready to make a deal yet, like the other places."

How did she know Haven wasn't close enough to the farm to be a threat? Lena's suspicions flashed heat then cold; a good guess, nothing more sinister. "We still need to know. And we have to survive the lesson to get home and warn them if Haven is a threat."

"We aren't discussing leaving," Mellow said. "We want to be safe, and that means not running away. You haven't been with us long enough to know how dangerous some places can be under a veneer of pleasantness. Or how a bad place can just be bad without being a threat. Now, how are we going to figure out the situation in a city without a high point for us to use?"

Anne shrugged and focused on the fire.

"What about a boat? Come in down the lake," Tik asked. "Maybe we can see what's happening at the harbor. It would be something."

"Or we try Scott's idea," Beattie said. "I know you don't want us to split up, but it's better than going in blind."

"Who would go?" Lena asked. She wasn't ready to change her mind about staying together, but a closed mind wouldn't solve the problem. And how many times in the past had their first view of a place told them it was dangerous? Maybe Anne had a point, and her abrasive attitude made it impossible to accept she was right?

"Beattie, me," Astrid said. "That's all. We leave everything behind and zip in and out."

"To get high enough you'll be climbing thirty, maybe fifty flights," Scott said. "That's not a fast option."

"And those stairs weren't kept clean even in the old days," Luis said. "You'll be breathing in dust and who knows what else. It will take hours, not minutes."

"So, it will be light when we get into place," Astrid said. "That's a good thing. We can come down the stairs before night and wait until it's dark enough to sneak out. A day, maybe a bit less."

That's if no one is guarding the buildings, Lena thought. If she was in charge at Haven, there would be people watching, not patrolling where they could be seen and ambushed. Hiding in the same buildings Astrid intended to use. People not exhausted from a long climb but stationed there for days. No one would be caught unawares. Peaceful or warlike, the inhabitants of Haven would be alert.

"I don't know if we have a good choice," she said. "Heading downriver means leaving the horses and coming back to a camp. Days, if we're lucky. Going inside to reconnoiter is dangerous. Even if Haven is a good place, being caught sneaking around doesn't say much about us."

"So, we go in without knowing?" Astrid said. "Slowly, right? Making sure we can run if we need to? With our weapons ready?"

"Tomorrow," Lena said. "We'll do just that. We bring everything with us. If we have to run, we cut the straps and drop the bags to let the horses run faster."

"I can support that," Anne said.

"We didn't ask for a vote," Astrid said.

18

They stayed the night far enough from Haven to make it unlikely they would be interrupted by anyone patrolling the edges of the community. Tomorrow they would go in, eyes open and weapons to hand.

"I seem to have made an enemy of Astrid," Anne said as she settled next to Lena on first watch.

"She's a teenager," Lena said. "That means you can be her mortal enemy one minute and her blood sister the next. She's getting used to being part of a family. Don't take it personally."

"If you say so," Anne said. "You know, I haven't heard this dream of yours. Just that you have one and it's the reason you hit the road. Mind telling me?"

This buddy version of Anne was a little disconcerting. She wasn't as young as Astrid, but she was almost as changeable. Lena poked at the embers and then added a few twigs to rekindle the flames. Keeping the fire going was a way to keep four-legged predators away, but too high a flame could attract two-legged ones and kill your ability to see into the dark.

She chose to engage Anne. "It's not going so well."

Her vision was no secret, and perhaps opening up to the woman would give her a better idea if she was a threat or just flaky. Da Vinci wouldn't have kept her around if she was the second, but maybe digging into the details of her supposed mission for Beta should wait for another day.

"I got that impression," Anne said. "We could make some tea. Maybe it will help pass the time."

"No cooking," Lena said, "but we can talk. Just keep it down so the others can sleep."

Anne looked around to check the sleeping bags. Lena waited for her to argue about keeping quiet, but she didn't. "Okay, so what's the story on your dream?"

It feels like a stupid idea now, Lena thought. "It's been long enough since the plagues burned out that people should be moved on from just surviving," she said. "I thought we could get people to agree to a few guidelines of behavior. Maybe cooperate in bringing back long-range communications. Safe roads. A new way to store and use energy."

"It would be good to be able to travel without much worry." Anne glanced back to where Luis was sitting with the horses. "Probably not with cars, right?"

"People like Da Vinci would take care of that," Lena said. "There are things like the handcarts for the railways, or electric cars. I mean, all that technology would still work if we could find a way to tailor it to what we have."

"And people traveled the country long before cars and railroads." Anne sounded wistful. "And radio might be easy. Mostly it's a power issue, right?"

Lena nodded as she let her mind float down the path she'd opened. "It will take years," she said. "Nature has already made some of the ideas far too much work. But the main problem, and what I see as the opportunity, is that making travel easier means the assholes, like the gang that's stealing kids, can move faster too. And drugs can be manufactured, and the kind of thing we saw in Liberty can happen all over again."

"Is that why people aren't signing up?"

Lena turned from gazing at the approach to their camp to look at Anne. Had she found the real reason just by listening?

"I mean, sure, lots of benefits. And good people usually like a few rules to keep things pleasant. But all that is theoretical, or far enough in the future to be hard to grasp. Gangs, flood, drought, disease, they are right in front of us."

"I never got much more than a 'no thanks', or a 'not yet,'" Lena said. "It never felt like I should ask for reasons. I'll give that a try, thanks for the idea."

"Or maybe someone is undermining you," Anne said. "Working for the people who prefer their victims separated and weak."

And there was the old Anne back. Lena didn't want to let her get any more digs in about loyalty. "I think it's unlikely. I'm probably a decade early on the ideas. When I was at home, I thought it would be easy, but I've learned better. We need to think about patrols and hired escorts for any travel that does happen. Have some of the ideas get closer to reality. Build out from my home more."

"But you have someone who used to do just that, work for the gangs. Before, I mean."

"Lots of survivors have pasts that they'd rather forget," Lena said. Anne was referring to Luis, but Tik was an ex-gang member. "There are too few of us now to keep judging people on their behavior before, or even during the plagues. What did you leave behind?"

"Small stuff. I liked to party. I never worked for a gang. I never hurt anyone." Anne glanced at Luis again. "He did, right? He told me he was a gang lawyer."

It was Luis' story to share, Lena thought. But she was surprised he'd done it with Anne.

"Protecting his kids," Lena said.

"He could be protecting them now," Anne said.

"They are dead. And don't tell me you think that's a lie. You need to drop all this, Anne. We can't keep traveling with you if you don't trust us."

Her body tensed and Anne poked at the fire as she thought about Lena's words. "So you'd leave me on the road?" she asked a few minutes later, her voice just above a whisper. "You know what that would mean."

"Not on the road. You haven't made any effort to learn how to survive alone, but if Haven is a good place, they can probably find you an escort. I need everyone around me on my side. On all our sides. Not someone looking for problems where there aren't any."

"I guess we should concentrate on guarding the camp," Anne said.

19

L ena sat on Bebop, looking at the entrance to Haven. They'd ridden a little over an hour through empty streets, following signs to the welcome center. Far from making her feel comfortable, the signs made Lena feel like she was being led to some holding pen.

The streets they passed were maintained, empty but not decaying. Greenery had taken over some of the buildings over the years, vines and grasses pressed against the glass walls from the inside and out. Someone had moved all the cars to the side, like they were parked and waiting to be driven away — or given a ticket for overstaying their time.

A closer look showed most of the vehicles had flat tires, some smashed windows, and open trunks. Haven was no Portland, with all the debris from the violence between Pearl Two and the gangs. Nor was it Glass House with its welcome signs. That was an agricultural center, not a city with businesses and residents and millions of inhabitants before the world changed.

"Are we going in?" Astrid asked. "They know we're here,

so this is probably our last chance to turn around and go somewhere else."

"It doesn't feel dangerous," Anne said. "It's empty up to now, but it's being taken care of, right? That means someone is in charge and they care about appearances."

To give her credit, Anne had tried for the entire day to be positive and not annoy anyone. It would take more than a few hours of the new Anne for anyone to believe it wasn't an act. But she had a point, Lena thought. Civic pride wasn't exactly the sign of violent gang activity.

"We stick together," she said, "but we go ahead. I think we need a concrete reason not to go in at this point."

She nudged Bebop to a walk. The welcome sign was hung across the road between two streetlights. No wall or fence closing off access around it, but it was clear they needed to go through, not around.

As they got closer, Lena saw people moving around half a block past the sign. No one was carrying arms. At least not ones large enough to be visible from so far.

A few adults walked with a long line of kids trailing behind. A daycare or preschool outing. Others carried packages from wagons to storefronts.

A few older kids ran along the streets, calling to each other in some game.

"Popcorn," Scott said, taking a deep breath. "And fried onions."

"There's a hot dog cart just down by that drugstore sign," Mellow said, "and nothing is broken. Like no one scavenged, ever. How is that possible?"

Luis moved up from the back. "Fixed stuff," he said. "There would be plenty of glass for materials, and bricks, whatever. That window on the store just past the sign isn't the original. The drugstore didn't likely have an oak door before."

His observation helped Lena ease the feeling that they were looking at the community equivalent of a rotten apple. Looks great on the outside but crawling with maggots on the inside. "I don't know if I'm just jaded but keep your eyes open. This could be a good place, like where we live, or... I don't know what but I'm not going to just accept this pretty picture."

The kids who'd been racing around turned and gave a feral howl.

"I guess we've been noticed," Mellow said. "Stop moving, we don't want to hurt anyone."

The kids were charging toward them, arms waving and grins spreading across slightly grimy faces. Bebop stutter stepped at the onrush and Lena reached down and patted him in comfort.

The crowd came to a halt in front of the horses, far enough to avoid startling them into running away. Six of them, all told, looking to be between seven and ten, all scruffy from running wild. She wondered why they weren't in school, or working. Perhaps it was Saturday?

"Welcome," the girl standing in the middle said. "We can take you in. Have you come from far away? Are you bringing trade goods? New candy maybe?"

"What's your name?" Luis asked.

"Lisa," she said. "You can get down and lead your horses. The stables are over on the west side, but they are welcome on the streets during the day."

"Our job is to lead new people in," a boy with red hair and a gap in his teeth said. "Most times no one comes, but now you are here and we get to do our job." His eyes lit up as Astrid dismounted. "Are you a real Viking?"

"As real as they get these days," she said. "Now, do you want to ride while you show us the way?"

She lifted the boy to Raven's back. "This is a real Indian pony."

The other kids begged for rides, and when each was sitting on a horse, Lisa told them to head four blocks before turning right.

20

Half an hour later, Lena realized the kids were leading them on a parade of their friends to show off the new visitors, and that they were allowed to ride horses. "Are we almost there?" she asked.

Lisa finished waving to a kid who was trimming a hedge in the park and then looked around. "Oh, yeah. It's on the next block. We can watch the horses while you go in. It will take a bit for you to get organized."

Or long enough for you to ride them around a bit more? Was it still a joy ride when there were four legs and a saddle involved?

"Is there somewhere we can tie them up?" Luis asked as if he'd read her mind. "I'm not sure they'll let you stop them if they smell food. Or something scares them."

They came to a stop outside what had been a chain restaurant. There was no hitching post, but streetlight poles still stood.

Lisa helped Anne and Luis secure the horses and then settled her team on the sidewalk to watch them. "We can give them something as a treat." She nudged one of the other girls. "Carrots? Apples?"

"Let me see," Lena said.

"We have them for this job," Lisa said. "Most visitors come on horses." The girl she'd nudged pulled out halved apples and cut-down carrots from a messenger bag.

"Do you know how to feed them?" Astrid asked.

"Yes," the boy who'd ridden Raven said. "Open hand and let them take it. If we lose a finger, it's our fault, not the horse's."

"Not too much," Lena said.

"Promise," Lisa said as she handed food to each child. "You go inside and someone will take over from us if you don't come out before our shift is over."

Beattie reached into her saddlebag. "What happens in there?"

"Questions," Lisa said. "No one is going to hurt you or jab you with needles. That's what some visitors think, anyway."

"Thank you for leading us here," Beattie said. "These are for you."

Lisa looked at the handful of honey candy in Beattie's hand. "Really?"

Beattie nodded. Lisa grabbed them like she was afraid it was a prank and Beattie would change her mind.

"I got them from Jack back in Novo Estes," she said. "Figured we'd run into some kids or an adult with a sweet tooth."

21

"Welcome." A woman stepped forward with her arms out as if she was going to hug everyone in the group. "My name is Sylvia. I hope your journey here wasn't too difficult."

Lena stayed in the middle of the group, letting Luis take the role of leader. Doing so let her observe, something she hadn't been able to do the times she was the spokesperson.

Observing might help identify the cause of the nagging feeling that something was wrong. What little they'd seen so far seemed pretty normal, but her inner paranoia wouldn't be silenced. Luis was the oldest of the group, and his past as a lawyer helped when he stepped into the role. He had a gift for getting people to drop their guards.

Anne was standing just behind her, so she couldn't see her reaction. A new place might just make a difference to the woman's attitude. And the plan was to leave her here. Not abandon her, but find a way to have Haven take her in. Even if it meant eventually escorting her to Beta. It might be good for the inhabitants of Haven to learn about Da Vinci's big plans, too.

"The road is never easy," Luis said, "but no worse than usual. Is this where we learn about Haven?"

"Yes, and if you are like many of our visitors, let me assure you it is not an indoctrination. When this is complete, you will be free to stay as visitors, temporary residents, or even work your way to permanent citizens."

"I guess we should get started," Luis said. "We don't want to break any rules by mistake."

Sylvia smiled widely and led them into a small side room, the kind used in the past for local group meetings, like the Lions or Rotary. Lena let the others get ahead of her, so she'd be sitting closest to the door and have Anne in front of her.

"This will be a short presentation from me," Sylvia said, "then you will have time to ask questions. Perhaps you'll feel comfortable enough to share your own stories, but no pressure."

The presentation was a series of poster boards with bulletin points. No pictures, and no real details. Sylvia spoke for about an hour, starting from just after the plagues to the founding of Haven.

The city had been hit hard like many of the others, closely packed people and insufficient infrastructure. The leaders had done their best to keep a community healthy by pulling the survivors into the center, but most of the inhabitants were bankers or other desk jobs. So, depression was their worst problem as people realized nothing they'd worked towards was ever going to come back.

"We traded with farms at the beginning," Sylvia said. "I was in PR before, so I got to use some of my skills. Food, and people to train us in how to turn the parks into farms. It took a long time, but we eventually became self-sufficient.

New people came, and that's when we had to introduce some guidelines."

She changed the poster board before continuing. This one held a hand-drawn map, kind of cartoony like at a tourist attraction. A large 'you are here' sticker in the center, with circles at different distances toward the edges. Lean craned her neck to read the clearest labels: farming, manufacturing, fishing.

"If you stay a while, you'll meet the various groups. This is simply an overview. The new people were of all different skills, backgrounds, and beliefs. Our first rule was that people could believe whatever they liked if they didn't try to force others to change. We had a few groups that couldn't manage the 'live and let live' idea. Now, we seem to have a great balance. People are committed to making this place live up to its name. A haven for all."

Sylvia may not be trying to recruit us, Lena thought, but she can't stop shining the place up. Although, how bad could a place be, with kids like Lisa's gang running around?

"What happens to the people who don't fit in?" Astrid asked.

"There are very few of them," Sylvia said. "If someone violates the few rules we have, they are brought in to explain. We need bodies, so we're not eager to exile anyone."

"And if they don't have a good explanation?" Beattie asked.

"They are encouraged to leave. Nothing too strong, but no one really wants to live in a place they aren't welcome."

Eventually they will run into someone more determined to change Haven than leave, or a gang with more power. Lena's questions could wait until later; she was watching the reactions in the room. Her companions were interested, and their questions were focused on finding the catch.

There would be one.

Anne didn't ask anything. Perhaps she is doing the same as me, Lena thought. If this is all true, then Anne should be eager to take the news home to Beta.

Lena admitted to herself, everything they'd seen up to now supported Sylvia's words. No one at the entrance seemed forced to do anything. The kids were healthy and inquisitive. Curiosity generally didn't thrive under a harsh regime.

"If we want to stay a while, is there a cost?" Lena asked. "I would like to get to know Haven more. Our home is a long way, but it's always a good idea to know your neighbors."

"I'm sure you've heard the same elsewhere," Sylvia said. "Work, trade, or a combination of both. That's pretty much the currency now. Here, we have a third option for temporary visitors: Stories. We're a bit starved for entertainment."

Lena wasn't quite ready to share their past with these people. "How long before we need to decide? If we're leaving, I'd like to do that before it gets dark."

"First night is free, but not all that comfortable. Space for you to camp near your rides. A share of the guard duty would be nice but not required."

"We should talk it out," Luis said. "How do we find you, or is someone else in charge of deciding who stays?"

"I'll be here a few hours." Sylvia ushered them out of the room. "If you decide to stay, I can point you to the job center. And if you commit to working, you get to stay in the hostel right away. Better than the cold ground, right?"

Outside, the kids were still watching the horses. More like petting them than standing on a real watch, but they were safe.

"Where can we settle for a bit?" Lena asked Lisa. "We need to grab a bite and rest our horses."

"At the stables," Lisa said. "We'll show you. It's not far, but it would be nice to have another ride."

The kids dismounted ten minutes later and then ran off yelling and laughing. The stables were newish. Built after the plagues, but sturdy. There was a large paddock for the horses to run with a handful already inside. Lena negotiated food and water for their horses and temporary storage for their packs. When that was done, they found a patch of grass not far away where they could talk privately.

22

The grass was well kept and clear of anything noxious. The aroma of horse and hay and something being cooked over a fire in the distance reached them as they sat. There was no doubt about staying, just how long and what they'd do with their time.

"We can work," Scott said. "I don't want to use our trade goods. I kind of hoped we'd take them to the farm. Have a little luxury, even if it's temporary."

"A week is enough, right?" Mellow asked. "If we'd been more observant, we would have known Pearl Two was wrong at the beginning. Maybe we wouldn't have left to spend the winter somewhere else, but we would have been cautious."

Lena carried a lot of guilt over her choice to remain in Portland. She should have noticed right away that Trixie's apparent kindness to Siren was grooming. The woman didn't treat anyone else that well. Most of the people who lived there were good, and Mellow was right. The choice wasn't to stay or leave, but Trixie made sure it felt like that.

And people changed after going through the trauma of

the plagues. As time passed, hopes for a new life were constantly killed. Survivor's guilt was normal now, not like before when there were counselors and medication to treat it. Look at Poorjohn. He started as a kind pastor to his flock of lost souls. Something eventually tipped him over to crazy megalomaniac. Maybe Trixie started out honestly wanting to make things better.

"We have to be purposeful about gathering intel," Beattie said, "not just try to make the best of something like we did in Portland. We work at it this time. Make an effort to look at all parts of the community."

"I can help with that," Anne said. "I can use my old marketing skills. I used to do a lot of audience research."

"You need to figure out what Da Vinci wants," Tik said. "We won't be here long no matter what we find."

"I can do both," Anne said, "then we can all tell Da Vinci what we saw. When you take me back, right? You are still taking me back?"

"It's out of our way," Astrid said. "Better you find some reason for these people to escort you back. Like, be an ambassador for Da Vinci."

"You would really leave me here?" Despite the discussion with Lena, Anne didn't seem convinced their relationship was over.

"We won't abandon you," Scott said, "but Da Vinci isn't expecting us to return. You have an obligation to do what he sent you out for."

If he really did, Lena thought.

Anne opened her mouth to argue her way into staying with them. But she didn't speak, simply shrugged and started picking at the grass.

"It would be faster if you found someone from here," Mellow said. "Our purpose is different, like Scott said. We might end up hanging out here for a long time if they are interested in Lena's ideas. Or we might start checking in on other communities on the way back north."

It was like they'd rehearsed it. Selling Anne on the idea she was making the decision to part ways. That it would be a benefit.

"We'll see," Anne said. "So, you are going to stick around for a while, at least? We can go through the job interviews together?"

"Let's see what that process is," Lena said. "Make your decision with enough information. I guess we should get back to Sylvia now. It's not that far to walk. I don't want to give her a chance to think we've left."

23

"I'm glad you came back," Sylvia said. "I'd like to introduce you to a few of the people who make Haven such a welcoming and safe place."

She ushered them back into the private room where five people sat drinking tea and talking. "These are the new people I mentioned," she said as she closed the door behind them.

Lena didn't recall hearing that new people were reported to the leadership. It made sense, but perhaps she'd been on the road too long because she suspected something more than just curiosity.

The leaders welcomed them and offered tea. "I'm Alice." The woman was older than Lena, possibly in her sixties. She pointed to the others. "Walter, Jean, Bud, and Frank. We are basically the core city managers."

"Good to meet you," Luis said. "We came to tell Sylvia we've decided to stay for a while. Probably do some contributing. Maybe look around for ideas to implement at home."

Frank glanced at Alice and then nodded. "Sylvia will find a spot in one of the hostels until you sign up for work."

"Will our things be safe?" Scott asked. "Is there a place to lock up our baggage? We don't have much of value, but we'd like to avoid heading home with nothing."

"It can be arranged," Sylvia said, "or you can lock things in the barn. You don't need to worry. Stealing is one of the few crimes we punish harshly. It's hard enough to get what we need to survive without losing it to someone feeling entitled."

That was new, Lena thought. Harsh punishment for infractions could explain how everyone was so determinedly happy. Or it could just explain why they were content to live in Haven. If your belongings were stolen in one of the rare circumstances, were they returned? She decided the answer could wait for another day.

"Is there a list of the rules?" Lena asked. "We're not planning on staying long, but life on the road doesn't make trust easy. I'd hate to break a law without knowing because we haven't been in a civilized place for so long."

"The hostel will have a handbook for you," Jean said. "It's not far from here. I'm in charge of the peace officers, so I have a good handle on the rules. I'm sure you'll be fine."

Sylvia held her arms out to usher them to the door, shutting down the discussion before it got too deep. Lena wondered if people usually didn't ask questions when they arrived or if it was something Haven discouraged. She wanted to believe Haven was what it seemed on the outside. But these five people hadn't exactly been forthcoming. Like she'd said, life on the road and all that. She'd been making it up to get more information, but it was likely truer than she realized.

"Before we go, can I talk to you?" she asked the leaders.

"Just a few minutes would be good. If not now, can we set up something?"

"Now is probably the best," Frank said. "Life here is busy, so you never know when we'll be together."

Sylvia left to arrange for more tea. The room wasn't big, but Lena wasn't about to let anyone out of her sight, so no one followed her. Haven was going to earn her trust. One lesson she'd learned, you couldn't trust the surface of any community. Pearl Two had seemed safe, and not just because Trixie had set up the gang attack to push them in.

24

"It might help to start with a bit of background," Alice said. "You've been on the road a long time, unless I'm mistaken."

"We met back in Liberty," Anne said. "I guess I've been traveling the least time."

Alice hadn't been looking at Anne when she spoke. She'd pegged Lena as the group leader despite Luis being the spokesperson.

"Anne's story is different from ours," she said. "I'll let her decide what she will tell you. You are right about the rest of us. Over a year. We came out to see what the country was like. We're heading home after this."

"I won't ask where your home is," Jean said. "Most people are protective about family left behind. I guess they are more precious than before."

"Okay, why don't we start with our history," Bud said. "My job is logistics, and librarian. My team looks ahead to see what we'll need in the next few months. You probably know Chicago had hot summers and cold winters. Nowadays, we need to make sure there's supplies to get through both. No AC means people are outside most of the summer. That's not possible in the winter."

"Where do you get things?" Astrid asked.

"Still a lot of stuff in warehouses," Bud said. "We head along the shore looking for what's been left. We have crafts-people who can weave and knit. Won't last forever, but we haven't needed to go much beyond our borders to scavenge."

It might explain why the local settlements didn't have much to say, Lena thought. Only one admitted to doing some trading with Haven. "So, is the city all Haven? Or are people all in a central place?"

"Both," Frank said. "I'm city planner. Means something different now. My job is to make things efficient, and plan for a bigger population. People have clustered by skills. Kind of like before when a wave of immigration happened. The people all moved close to each other until they settled and felt safe enough to move out."

"How many?" Tik asked. "If you are managing to keep the peace, and do more than barely survive, they can't be too far apart."

"Very observant," Jean said. "Nothing in Haven is more than an hour's walk from any other enclave. From here, what we think of as the center, the farthest out is the clothing community. Merely because of the smell. Tanning and dying are particularly pungent."

"If we wanted to visit some of these places, would we need permission?" Lena asked. "We might have some tips from other communities or perhaps learn a few things."

"Your free time is your own," Alice said. "Our crafts-people love to talk shop."

"I guess I might have some time," Anne said. "I don't know what Beta might need to learn from here. I can do that on my own."

Alice smiled at Anne as though she'd offered something of value. "You must tell us about Beta. It sounds like we have a lot in common with them. Of course, our technological work is all practical."

"What have you found on your travels?" Walter asked. "We need a bit of news for the paper. My job, I guess I should say, is communications. Vital so no group feels isolated and starts to cause trouble."

"Like Lena said, we came to see what the wider country is like," Tik said. "See if it's safe to start thinking about building alliances. Make the road safe, if they're still passable."

"They're thinking of building alliances," Anne said. "Make a country again. Safe roads, trade, allies in fighting some gang we encountered."

Lena wished Anne would stick to her own story rather than blab all their secrets. She'd hoped to see more of Haven before bringing up alliances. If it was what it seemed, Haven would be a good partner. If not, like most places, they would be a bad enemy.

"I see," Alice said. "And what did you learn?"

"I'm sure you can guess," Lena said. "Good places, bad places. Like Anne said, there's a gang operating up north. Taking kids to the towns up on the border with Canada. Trying to repopulate by stealing them away."

"Not new behavior for humans. Taking what they want rather than working for it," Frank said. "There's opposition? How effective?"

"West coast," Astrid said. "People are fighting back. We don't know how successful they are. At Liberty, they're trying since we kicked out the gangster who took over."

"I'll have to think about the wording on this," Walter

said. "People need to know, but I don't want them running scared."

So, there was some spin going on. Lena tried to set it aside because she'd be doing the same thing. Making sure bad news didn't cause panic. She was going to look at Haven with a more critical eye than she had other places, but not everything was a red flag.

"Look out for missing kids," Astrid said. "That's the first sign. You follow up on anyone who disappears, you'll find out if it's the gang. I'm pretty sure they're too busy to expand right now."

"Thank you," Alice said. "It's good to know what might be a threat. And have you made any alliances?"

"I think it's too early," Lena said. "Or maybe, just talking about it is good enough. Some places are shutting out the world and others just don't see the value right now."

"Shutting out the world won't work," Frank said. "All it does is leave you alone when the bad guys come for you. Or really bad weather, or sickness. It's always something. Life has never been easy since we first crawled out of the mud and stood on two legs."

"I don't think we are ready to sign agreements with strangers," Bud said, "but Frank has a point. Just because we don't have walls doesn't mean we're exactly open to new ideas."

Another maybe.

Lena let the topic go. Until she was sure about Haven, there was no point in trying to discuss the subject. "I think we should go get settled. We'll want to check out the lockers at the stable for a longer-term option."

"You can inquire about work tomorrow at the center," Alice said. "Anyone will show you the way. I wonder, Anne,

if you could spare a few moments to talk about your home?
You can join your companions at the hostel."

25

"It's temporary, don't unpack anything," Lena said when they got to the hostel. "We need to be ready to head out at any time, without leaving anything behind."

The hostel was clean and had been a Holiday Inn before the plagues, so Lena's fear that they would be in bunks and only common spaces with shared bathrooms and all their belongings clutched to their chests was for nothing. Leaving the door open between their rooms gave enough space for everyone to claim a little privacy. And two rooms meant two bathrooms.

"While Anne isn't here, we should talk," Luis said.

"Maybe she'll take a job with a group far from us," Astrid said. "I didn't like that she told them about us. I don't know if it was because she has no boundaries, or if we should be worried about her."

Lena didn't add her agreement to the general grousing. No one was in the mood to defend her, but harping on about Anne's shortcomings wasn't productive.

"We should pick jobs that don't separate us like in Pearl

Two," Beattie said. "We need to get a good idea about their peacekeepers but not take on full time shifts. Maybe only one of us needs to apply there."

"It's possible no one will offer that kind of job to a stranger," Scott said. "I agree we should be working similar shifts, but maybe we keep our specialties as quiet as possible."

"I don't think Beattie and Astrid are going to pass as babysitters," Mellow said, then ducked a jab from Astrid. "Come on, even that kid knew enough to see you as a warrior."

"I guess we do stick out," Astrid said. "We'll find a way to deal with it. But I was thinking maybe we try to work in pairs. Me, Tik, Beattie can all fight, but they don't know that. If I try for some guard duties, it leaves the other two for backup. Like Lena and Tik, Scott and Luis, Beattie and Mellow?"

"And if Anne needs to be covered?" Luis asked.

"You mean protected or watched?" Astrid asked.

"Either? Both?" Luis pulled out the sofa bed. "I'm good here."

"Leave Anne until she gets here," Lena said. "Our job over the next few days is to gather intelligence. I'm not just going along with the official story this time."

Anne arrived an hour later with an armful of sandwiches and a bag of sodas. "Our meal for tonight," she said. "After this we need to pay like everywhere else, work or trade goods."

Tik and Scott dragged the coffee tables into the room Lena had picked as their base.

"Like a little dining room," Anne said. "So, what have you decided?"

"We'll look for jobs tomorrow," Mellow said. "What about you? Did Alice tell you anything after we left?"

"I told her about Da Vinci and Beta. She might send an envoy, but that's up to them. If it's soon, I can tag along to get home." She opened the sandwich wrappers and laid them out as a tablecloth. "I went to the job center. It's not far. I thought if I got an idea what's needed, we could go for jobs we want."

And there was the hole in their great 'pretend we're not who we are' plan. Anne knew all their skills.

"Did you get a list?" Mellow asked. "We all thought we'd try something new here. I'm kind of burned out as a medic."

"You could work the crèche," Anne said, "or teach the younger grades. Lena, you can be a teacher too."

"I can do other things," Lena said. "Maybe if you tell us what you found out, we can decide on our first choices so it's less pressure tomorrow."

"It's all kind of grunt work," Anne said. "It's probably going to be different every day. Haven is big enough to cover most of the critical work."

"Grunt work never hurt anyone," Luis said. "Working in the stables might get us free storage."

"Or you could work with Jean. I saw a posting for a few days of clerking. You were a lawyer, right?"

"So, there was no list of usual vacancies," Lena said. "I guess we'll figure it out tomorrow. Did you sign up for anything?"

"I saw something about working with the archives," she said. "I might have to stay close to the job. But, like you said, let's wait until tomorrow. I know Astrid and Beattie won't want to muck out stables, right?"

"How do you know?" Astrid said. "Being a warrior doesn't mean you don't shovel shit every once in a while."

Anne picked up a sandwich and a bottle of soda. "Sorry, I didn't mean anything by that. I thought I was helping by scouting out the opportunities."

"You know, we're all tired," Lena said. "Let's use the chance to sleep on a nice bed tonight. No need to set a guard. We have the key, and we can barricade the doors with chairs."

"Not when you aren't here," Anne said. "Just the key then."

"Let it be," Lena said. "If we try to be completely safe, we'll be paralyzed. Our supplies will be fine. Let's decide on what we're going to do."

I am not leaving anyone in the rooms as a guard. A sure way to tip off whoever is interested that we don't trust the people in Haven. Or that we have something worth the risk of getting caught stealing.

IN THE MORNING, Anne signed up for the job with the Archives group and headed out before any of the others had even looked at the opportunities.

"We need to store our stuff in the stables," Lena said when they were alone. "I don't like it, but I can't do what is needed if I'm worried we'll lose everything to a thief or be stuck here to deal with a conviction."

"Anne doesn't need to know," Luis said. "She took her stuff this morning. We can leave her share of the trade goods in the room. And I'm going to ask about other options. The stable is a little too deep into Haven for a fast escape if we need it."

An hour later they'd all been assigned work; Luis and Mellow to the stables, Lena and Beattie to work in a garden tending vegetables, Astrid and Scott to a building lot. Tik joined a scavenging team working the warehouses. While she'd preferred they all pair off, there was an odd number of them, and Tik volunteered to the scavenging crew.

"See you at the hostel for dinner," Lena said as they broke off to their assignments.

26

E veryone was hot, dirty and worn out from work when they met in the lobby of the Holiday Inn hostel. Lena suggested they hold off on discussions until everyone showered and changed. Anne was waiting in the first bedroom, already cleaned up when Lena opened the door, so there was no opportunity to discuss their real plans anyway.

"How was your day?" Lena asked. "The archives must be fascinating."

"Interesting is more like it," Anne said. "They need me to go back, a week of work at least, so I should probably move out."

"You've decided to stick around and find someone else to escort you home?" Astrid asked. "We'll miss you."

It sounded flat to Lena's ears, but Astrid added a smile so maybe Anne would believe her.

"Your stuff is here," Astrid said. "A share of the trade stuff, and your personal bags."

"Thanks," Anne said, looking around. "Your stuff is in storage?"

"Yes," Lena said. "We'll leave Beau for you in the stables if we leave before we see you."

No matter how suspicious she was of Anne, Lena wouldn't leave her without a horse. Walking to Beta would likely end in her death by the end of the first day, either by accident or some wild animal attack. Buying another horse, or borrowing one, would leave the woman in debt she might never pay off.

Anne picked up her pack and the second saddlebag full of goods. "I guess I can head out now," she said, looking around as if waiting for someone to ask her to stay. "They have a barracks at the archives, so I can bunk there. Please don't leave without saying goodbye."

"You know where we are," Astrid said. "No reason you can't visit. You shouldn't be out after dark, right? So have a good time here, and I hope you get what you need."

Anne took one more look around and then sighed. "Good luck to you, too."

"We can finally talk," Scott said as he came out of the bathroom drying his hair. "It was getting really hard to pretend we weren't planning things behind her back."

"Don't relax too much," Luis said. "We won't always be alone. So, what did everyone find out?"

A knock on the door stopped any further conversation. Tik looked through the peephole and then opened the door. Sylvia stood in the hallway. "I have an apartment for you," she said. "You came along just as we needed someone to try out this living experiment. It's part of your payment for work." She held up a set of keys. "Not too far away. Four bedrooms, three bathrooms. Yours until you decide to leave." She passed Lena a handful of keys. "Copies for every-one. Would you like to come now?"

.   .   .

THE APARTMENT MUST HAVE BEEN worth a couple of million dollars before. A penthouse suite with a view over the city, and a large terrace rather than just a balcony.

"This is too much for just a week or so's worth of labor," Scott said.

"We only have a handful of buildings ready for occupation," Sylvia said. "You're doing us a favor by living here. Call it a shakedown period. The plumbing is all gravity supplied. The twenty-floor walk-up is a bit of a journey, but no one has figured out a manual elevator for more than three floors."

The explanation was reasonable, but it still didn't seem right. Lena took in the view and the comfortable furnishings. And they were the only people living on the floor, so privacy wasn't an issue. They were all healthy enough to manage the climb up, and electronic snooping was a thing of the past. If anyone wanted to keep tabs on them, they would need to be in the room.

"Is anyone else living here?" she asked.

"Each floor has one occupied suite," Sylvia answered. "A real trial of the idea of repopulating the empty buildings."

"Thanks," Luis said. "It's nice to have our own bedrooms for a change. Not used to much generosity these days. Who do we report our experience to when we leave?"

"Me. I'll compile everyone's feedback for the leaders. I hope it works out; having more living space will make it easier for us to take in more refugees."

Lena tossed the small backpack Luis had left her when he put their belongings in storage onto the kitchen counter. Everyone had enough for two or three days on them. Tonight's meal could come from their travel food, so they didn't need to climb the stairs again.

"Okay, so there's a grill on the terrace," Sylvia said. "We're still working on getting a stove working. The other tenants will be doing takeout, but if you try cooking outside, it would help immensely. I'll leave you to it."

Lena showed her out the door and watched as the woman entered the stairwell.

"Can we pretend for one night this is all good?" Mellow asked. "One night of enjoying before we try to figure out the catch?"

"I think that's a great idea," Lena said. "We can share our observations while we eat. Just keep our voices down. The people below might have their windows open."

"At least Anne can't drop by," Mellow said. "She doesn't even know where we are."

Lena didn't expect anyone in Haven to think twice about telling Anne where they were, or she'd track them down at work.

A worry for tomorrow. It will be nice to be by ourselves tonight.

Scott worked the grill but only as a stove top. They didn't have any fresh meat to char over the flames. The main difference between a campfire and this metal contraption was they wouldn't need to worry about the danger of forest fire when they were done.

"There was a basket in the kitchen," Mellow said. "A bottle of wine, and a bag of chocolate. The chocolate is stale, but still a treat."

Standards were lower these days, Lena thought. Before the plagues, the sweets would have been tossed out in favor of fresh ones. Of course, chocolate, like coffee, grew so far away that no one would waste any now.

"So, the plan?" Astrid asked. "We need to be careful about asking questions, but we are still going to do it, right?"

The wine was a little raw in Lena's mouth. Someone had a long way to go before they could produce a good vintage, but she'd had worse. "Before we do, what kind of surveillance do you think Sylvia could have put on us?"

27

"I'll have a look around," Tik said. "Nothing out here unless, like you said, the people downstairs can hear us."

"I'll come," Astrid said. "I need to know what to look for in the future, right? Soldiers can be trained in spying, too. How come you know this stuff?"

They walked out of earshot as Tik explained how his old boss Basso would set up listening posts.

"I think we need an escape plan," Luis said. "Something flexible. If we have to run, we don't want to leave everything behind. So, a couple of places where we can pick up a portion of our stuff. And no one leaves anything here that they can't do without."

"The horses," Beattie said. "There's a couple of stables, but would it look suspicious if we separated them? And would it be useful to have only some of us on horseback?"

"There's a corral in the parking garage," Scott said. "I noticed the door to the garage was unlocked. So, you know, I looked. We could bring them here. Then, make sure we need to ride to our assignments. Keep our essentials in saddlebags, the rest we could haul up here."

Lena wondered if it was worth the effort. Twenty stories was hard enough with just a daily backpack. If they brought up the supplies, it would mean several heavy trips. "Could we leave everything with the horses?"

"Maybe sell the idea as a part of the shakedown," Luis said. "People living here permanently wouldn't want their things stored somewhere else. I'll talk to Sylvia tomorrow. Astrid and I are assigned to the stables again. Easy for us to move everything back if she buys it."

"So every day we take the absolute essentials with us in case we leave without coming back," Beattie said.

"I'm going to visit other communities starting tomorrow," Lena said. "Who wants to come?"

"You and I can work the garden in the morning," Scott said. "We'll have to clean up there, but then we'll have a few hours to travel. Where were you thinking?"

Before Lena could answer, Tik and Astrid returned.

"The people downstairs are either not home or very quiet," Astrid said. "They might have a balcony or an open window right under this terrace, so we should be cautious."

"If there are ways to hear us, then we'll hear them," Tik said, "if they really are a family testing out the viability of living in high rises and not just a single spy. It's impossible to tell yet whether we can trust anything we're told."

"Let's play it like we do," Mellow said. "Trust them, I mean. Otherwise, we might tip them off."

"Agreed," Lena said. "I don't want to range too far on our first visit. The population here can't be living off the yield of the small gardens. So, where are the rest of the farms?"

"I know how to get to them," Scott said. "Like Sylvia said,

not much more than an hour's ride. We'll be back for dinner and a report."

"So, everyone act like we're not spying, but spy our hearts out?" Astrid asked with a laugh. "I guess Beattie and me should leave our obvious weapons here, then. In the apartment. We can make it upstairs pretty fast if we need to."

"No," Beattie said. "We'll scout for a better place now. Didn't these buildings come with storage?"

How had she thought of that when Luis and I didn't, Lena thought. "In the basement. I'd guess somewhere around the elevator stack. We have those padlocks we got from Costco. That's the answer to our storage."

"As long as we are together. Only two keys," Beattie said.

"In an emergency, we can break the lock with something heavy," Tik said. "I'll come with you now. It's not too late to get our stuff from the stables. And we can leave an axe just outside the locker for a fast escape."

Youth went a long way to ignoring the number of stairs they'd have to travel. Lena felt a pang at the idea she was too old to keep up with the rest. At least she had company with Luis, who might be wiry, but he was older than her.

"Tomorrow," she said. "We should take advantage of having bedrooms and get rest so we can be on alert tomorrow. I don't want to be wondering what the catch is here for too long. The first sight of something wrong, we leave."

_____

28

Working the closer garden in the morning was less strenuous than Lena feared. The crop was all lettuce and tomatoes. Produce that didn't need to be stored. The daily yield would likely satisfy demand. And along with salad stuff, there were raspberry canes and strawberries, but the season was well passed for those.

"Wash up over in the restroom block," the man who'd supervised their morning shift said at lunch. "Good work. We could use you tomorrow."

"We'll see," Scott said. "Might need a day of rest. Riding isn't the same thing as turning soil and picking leaves."

The area had been a park before being turned into a small farm. Someone had rigged showers in one of the toilet stalls. It was awkward but better than going home. Lena pulled out the change of clothes she'd brought for the trip. What if the visit included working? She sighed and changed. Tonight, she'd suggest they wash their spare clothes, a luxury they didn't get much on the road. Washing in a stream didn't quite do the same as a hot soak in soapy water.

Scott was waiting for her with Bebop and Beauty ready to travel. "We can talk about it on the way," he said. "Our goal. I mean, it's not just for a chat about farming, right?"

She mounted and followed him down the side street that led to a main road.

"I want to walk away with a better feeling about Haven," she said. "It's a big place, and they could put five hundred people on the road in days. Unless we know well in advance they are coming, we'd be lost. I don't want to have to put lookouts on the roads. I don't think any of our allies do either."

"I agree about the risk," he said. "We don't even know if they already have people scouting for victims. Or even if Sylvia told us the truth about the number of people. I miss the days on the farm where we only worried about the weather and planting schedules."

She nudged Bebop to his side. His words reminded her that people were missed more than the days before the plagues. Regular life meant you lost people, even if it was temporary. "Do you regret coming out?"

"We needed to know. I'm glad you and Mellow joined us. If it was just Tik and me, we might not have gone as far because we missed the two of you. And we wouldn't know Beattie or Astrid, or Luis. I can't really imagine being without them now."

The farm will be better for the new blood, too.

Lena rode in silence for a while, thinking about the future. No matter what they learned about Haven, they would be home in a few months. Back to worrying about the day-to-day running of a farm and meeting the terms of the agreements with their neighbors. Sleeping in a bed every night, cooking on a wood-fired stove and sitting around at night chatting.

"What do you think we should look out for?" she asked. "It's a farm, so we should notice if it's being run for the community we've been told about."

"And not stocking up to feed an invading army?" He laughed. "I don't think it will be obvious."

"So, we go in as if we're looking for new farming techniques and willing to share what we know. Keep our eyes open for inconsistencies. A couple of hours and we leave." It might work for this visit, but how would they know if a fishing enterprise was hiding a secret, or a clothing sorting operation?

"Fingers crossed," he said. "I don't know if we'll ever truly trust strangers again, but next visit you'll have more information. I won't come, but Mellow is good at catching things, Luis will have a wide range of knowledge. Just..."

"Not Astrid? Or Beattie? Neither of them can hide their skills. What about Tik?" She didn't want to cut anyone out, but Scott had a point. Going into a conversation looking like you could fight your way out wasn't the best way to build trust.

"They should do their own investigating," Scott said. "I guess I should say, they are doing it. Tik was signing up to go with the peacekeepers today. Suss out their capabilities and authority. Our warriors were going to do some street cleaning, so they get to snoop around."

"Tik shouldn't go on his own," she said. "Yeah, I know we're an odd number. I guess he shouldn't always be the one who doesn't have a partner."

"That's a conversation for tonight," Scott said. "Our destination is a few blocks away."

The people working the farm were in the fields under

wide-brimmed hats, with water buckets spaced along the rows.

A cluster of people stood at the side of a wagon listening to a woman issuing orders. The fields in the distance were full of yet unripe crops.

"A month until harvest," Scott said. "Not sure it will be enough for the whole city unless they have reserves."

"Let's find out," Lena said as she nudged Bebop toward the wagon.

"Good to meet new people," the man in charge of the workers said. He waited until they dismounted and reached to shake Lena's hand. "Isaac. And you?"

Lena made the introductions. "We have a farm up north," she said. "Different cycles, by the look of it."

"We're lucky we have a lot of workers. Keeping the weeds down and looking for parasites. In a month we'll have three times as many people harvesting."

"Will it be enough?" Scott asked. "For the winter? We don't have as many to feed, but our crops get hit by weather or bugs often enough."

Not exactly true. Everyone at the farm worked hard to make sure the crops were healthy enough to survive a storm or two.

Isaac chewed his lip and stared out over the crops. "Still worry, without the hardier seeds from before, our crop is subject to the old problems. We don't have all the chemicals, but we also have more hands. It's good to keep an eye out. And we've managed to rig some irrigation systems with hand pumps. More targeted than before, so better for the soil. Less erosion."

"We don't have the piping for much," Scott said. "I'd love to see how you built the system. Maybe we can scavenge what we need on the way home."

Isaac was happy to show them his improvements, most of which they had at the farm. But playing at needing help was a good way to get him talking.

Lena lagged behind to engage one or two of the other people, but they excused themselves, saying they needed to refill the water buckets.

By the time they left, Scott had a set of drawings and list of items to scavenge for two ideas to use at the farm. Although, in the time they'd been away, who knows what Keith or Evan had invented.

Nothing stood out as wrong, exactly. No subjects discussed that gave them an idea of Isaac's plans or orders.

Lena didn't feel any less suspicious as they rode back to the apartment.

29

Another dinner on the terrace. As she climbed the stairs to the apartment, Lena realized it would be easy to trap anyone inside by barricading the exits. Lena wished she could just accept Haven at face value, but she wasn't the only one with a creeping feeling about the place.

On the nineteenth floor, she peeked at the apartment doors. No sound came through the closed units, and Lena knew that was not normal. Noise leaked out in the most well-made buildings. They still couldn't take their privacy for granted. No matter what Sylvia said. This apartment was too good for anyone who was passing through.

"I'll be happy sleeping on the ground again when we leave," Luis said. "You know, we never really worried about it before, but anyone living higher than the emergency ladders could reach were doomed in buildings like this."

"I'm trying not to think about it," Mellow said. "I guess we can add it to our assessment of the place for Sylvia. It doesn't feel normal to be living this far off the ground."

"Do we need to tell her what we think?" Astrid asked. "I

mean, when we want to leave, why should we delay for her? And who says their experiment isn't some excuse to trap us up here?"

"We'll write up something," Tik said. "That way, she gets what she said she needs and we can just go without raising suspicions."

Lena wasn't sure what she'd put on the paper. It's a nice view, but it's not going to work for a lot of people with the stairs. And having running hot and cold water isn't worth it if you have to cook outside all year round. "So, what was everyone's day like?"

"Tell us about the farms," Luis said. "You probably learned more than us."

"What we saw was pretty normal," Scott said. "Not enough for the whole city, but Isaac said they have another two farms nearby. I don't know that we learned anything to help work out what kind of community this is."

"The people with Isaac were very reluctant to talk," Lena said. "So, I'm still worried we're missing something big."

"How badly do you need to know?" Beattie asked. "I get that having an unknown threat this close to home is a problem. But think about it. If we do find something wrong, will we be allowed to go? Or do you think we'll find what we need and no one will notice?"

The idea of being chased as they left was more than unsettling. If it happened, they couldn't go home and lead a threat to their families. Haven could raise an overwhelming force. The local communities would pull together, but they'd only just beaten Newton Cole, and he only had a handful of fighters.

Their remaining option would be to keep leading pursuers away from their home.

"If we leave without knowing, we will always think of it

as a threat," Luis said. "I think we look a bit harder. A couple more days. We've got everything here, so packing up for the road will be fast."

They cleaned up the remnants of dinner and took the dishes inside. In the kitchen, Lena helped Mellow to wash up while the others settled in the living room.

"Did you learn anything?" she asked Mellow quietly.

"Nothing. But I'm with you. This is too good given everything we've encountered along the way. I'm not saying it can't be real, but I think we should leave soon."

"Maybe I'm just being paranoid," Lena said. "We can decide tomorrow. Maybe set a limit on our time here."

"A deadline might help," Mellow said, "and a couple more visits."

30

Lena changed the subject when she rejoined the group in the living room. "What's the thing you'll miss most when we get home?" she asked.

"New people," Mellow said. "I know we've met some we could live without, but we've seen different ways of living. And not all of them are bad. Even in the worst places, we got benefit."

"Trixie had some good ideas," Astrid said, "about protection, not selling kids. Maybe we can't use them at the farm exactly, but I bet there are ways to improve what we're doing."

"No walls, and no roaming gangs," Mellow said, "but Pearl Two had a lot of natural medicine knowledge. I'll be using some of the recipes I got from the clinic."

Lena let the conversation drift into the background as she thought of her own answer to that question. It was easier to think about what she wouldn't miss, but that wasn't the reason she'd asked. It would be eighteen months away from home before they returned. There were good things and good people in that time.

Pearl Two might end up being what Trixie pretended it was with a better leader. Eventually, Greenly would come out of the mountains. Even Nicolette kept her people happy. Sure, it was with drugs and cosmetics, but she didn't make people stay, and no one had been forced to join her. Well, maybe she didn't get enough practice on that part.

Towns like Virtue worried her, but their strict rules and old-fashioned outlook meant they would stay as closed communities. The narrowness of their view wouldn't attract enough people to form a threat to anyone.

"Poly tunnels," Scott said. "We'll be working on them, maybe keep our eyes out for the makings on the way home."

His comment was so close to her thoughts about finding the good in a bad situation that Lena wondered if she'd spoken aloud.

"I guess we should think about what to look for as we go," she said. "That pump mechanism might come in handy for more than just irrigation. And we should stop at Beta to give Da Vinci the notes."

"I guess that means we should talk to Anne before we go," Astrid said.

"Da Vinci doesn't know we met up," Luis said. "Do we really need to mention her?"

Keeping quiet about Anne seemed a little too deceptive. They had time to talk it through on the road. Letting Anne know they were leaving would open the door for her to join them. The last couple of days without her niggling little remarks had been a relief.

"Was that the door?" Tik asked. "Someone came all the way up here?"

Lena went to check. She'd heard the knock too but couldn't imagine why someone would climb up for a chance to visit.

"It's Anne," she said after checking the peephole.

"Did we summon her?" Astrid asked. "Like, we said her name and she appeared?"

Lena waved her to silence. They couldn't pretend to be out because Anne would have heard them. And she might have checked to see their horses down in the garage. In fact, she probably had to save walking up all those stairs if they were out.

She opened the door and stepped aside for Anne to enter.

"I thought I'd see how you are settling in," Anne said. "Nice apartment."

"It's okay," Astrid said. "What have you been doing?"

"Working to get some old books sorted out," Anne said with a shrug. "The Archivist thinks we'll find old records on how people managed in the days before technology. There were some Amish records, but I wasn't allowed to read them."

"Are you staying?" Lena asked. "For a while?"

"Yeah. I guess Da Vinci will want the information I can find. I asked if I could read the records in my spare time. Are you guys hanging around?"

"For a few days," Luis said. "Lots of things to explore around here. I'd kind of given up on the idea of a big city working so well."

"You know, the good weather won't hold forever," Anne said. "You'd learn a lot more if you stuck around through winter. I found out they do a lot of teaching and studying when it's too cold to work outside."

"We can still make it home if we leave in the next few weeks," Lena said. Did Anne know they were spying? Or was she trying to get them to stay long enough to escort her home? "We could drop in on Beta to give them any news you want to share."

Anne walked to the window to look over the view. "It's okay, they aren't expecting updates."

"Not even that you are still alive, and that your companions died?" Mellow asked.

"Da Vinci wants results, not news," Anne said. "Did you check with Sylvia about your timing?"

"I didn't know we had to," Tik said. "She seemed pretty relaxed about the whole thing."

"I guess," Anne said. "I got to look through the almanacs. There's probably a big storm coming."

"How accurate are they?" Mellow asked. "And what kind of storm? Did the farmers look like they were worried, Lena?"

Anne turned back to look at everyone and with the view of Chicago behind her. She reminded Lena of public speakers making a huge announcement. "The almanacs aren't so specific, sometime between now and a couple of weeks," she said. "I thought I'd mention it if you are planning on being on the road. You'll want to find shelter."

"Thanks. We'll keep it in mind. Is this news the rest of Haven knows?" Lena hadn't noticed any preparations earlier, and if the leaders relied on almanacs, they should have been talking about the harvest being in danger.

"I don't know. I'm just doing clerking work." Anne stepped back into the room and headed for the door. "If you stick around, I can bring you more news."

"Thanks for the offer," Beattie said. "I guess we'll let you know when we decide."

Anne shrugged like she didn't expect anything from them. "Sure. I've got a long ride back, so goodnight."

Lena watched Anne enter the stairwell and waited to

make sure she didn't sneak back into the lobby and put her ear to the door.

"That was weird," Astrid said. "She could have dropped by while we were working to tell us about the weather. But she came all the way up here."

"And her comment about Da Vinci?" Tik said. "That's not what I got from him. Only wanting results? No way. He was all about the information."

"It was about trying to get us to stay longer," Luis said. "Someone guessed we're already planning to leave."

Or someone overheard us talk about it. Lena kept her suspicions to herself.

31

I t took two days to get time for another visit. Lena and Astrid left the apartment building early in the morning to ensure they would arrive at the clothing department with enough time to explore all the aspects if the wanted to find the truth. The reason the department was so far from where most people lived became obvious as they got close.

"Oh, that is the worst smell," Astrid said. She dragged a scarf from her saddlebag and tied it into a mask. "Barely better, but I guess I can keep going."

Lena pulled her bandana up over her mouth and nose before saying, "There's a worse smell, but you are too young remember, I guess."

"Dead people?" Astrid asked. "Lots of them."

"Rotting people," Lena said. "I guess the workers here get used to reek of the dye pots and tanning baths."

"It's hard to believe clothes don't smell of it," Astrid said.

"Ever smelled new leather?" Lena stifled the chuckle, not wanting to draw in any more foul air than necessary.

The administration and distribution center was in a

large warehouse close to the old highway. The directions Lena received were clear, and Sylvia had promised the actual odorous work was done another half-hour ride from the building. "If the wind is in the right direction, you can hardly smell it."

The wind was not in the right direction.

"Sylvia sent a note to say you'd be here," a woman said as she hustled them inside. "Your horses will be taken by our grooms. I'm sure you'll feel better in here."

"Marielle," the woman said. "My name. And you must be Astrid, and Lena?" Marielle held out her hand to shake, clearly knowing which was which. Sylvia must have sent descriptions, too.

"Right," Astrid said. "We're looking to see if anyone has new ideas on production. We usually scavenge clothing or weave up from something we find in a craft store."

"Tea?" Marielle asked. "It will clear out the taste of our processes. I promise it's a special blend just to keep us from being sick all over the place."

They accepted, and Marielle led them to a small office. "I'll take you around the warehouse a little later," she said. "Perhaps you can tell me what your challenges are?"

"We're hoping to move on from scavenging," Lena said.

This was the story they came up with to cover their snooping. Anne's visit simply amplified the feeling they were being watched. The lie played well because stuff was running out, or decaying. At some point in the very near future, everyone would be making their own everything or doing without.

"If we don't want our home to stink, is it possible?" Astrid asked. "We'll need leather, but if we don't dye our clothes will it be better?"

"Most of it is the leather," Marielle said, waving to the

outside. "Sorry, you need a lot of strong solutions to break it down to where it can be worked."

"We might want to trade with someone for leather," Lena said, "but I don't know if we're there yet. I was hoping to get ideas on better distribution? Or maybe shearing and spinning, or processing flax. I don't really know exactly."

"I'm sure there are books around," Marielle said. "We started with the chemicals we could find, but they didn't last. At least urine and things like animal brains are easy to source. How big is your community?"

The question was probably innocent, but every time someone tried to find information about her home, Lena's skin prickled in warning.

"Not as big as Haven," Astrid said. "Where would we find books?"

"In Haven? The archives, but if you pass a library or maybe a college on your way, you should find what you need. I hear those places were spared the worst of the looting. Can't eat books."

"Can we see your operation?" Lena asked. "I guess you have a lot of things from the warehouses at the lake and some of the trucks and ships that were making deliveries?"

Marielle stood and gestured toward the door. "The supplies are running low now, just like you said. Too much time has passed for us to keep relying on what was left behind. More people means the stores we have go faster, too."

She handed them masks. "Lots of lint and fine thread in the air," she said. "We keep the ventilation as good as we can, but only high-powered extraction fans would make unprotected breathing safe inside."

She opened a door that separated what was basically a lobby from the working area. The warehouse was separated into several sections, all parts of the process of turning fiber into clothing.

"We shear our sheep and other wool-bearing animals and bring it all cleaned to my section. The fiber is picked and washed near the dye pits. No need to spread any of the odor around. Then it's brought here for carding, spinning and weaving."

As they walked through sections, Lena could see it was in logical order. Spinning at the front, handing back to weaving, then cutting and finally sewing. The looms reminded her of working in the women's house at Virtue. It was a much larger scale here, so was the demand. And in Virtue, the looms didn't fill the air with dust and lint like it did here.

"You don't knit?" she asked. "Scarves, hats, socks?"

Marielle pointed toward the right wall. "Another building. We need them, Haven gets mean winters. I guess having so many people die will have some effect on that global warming thing, but it's going to take more than my lifetime to see it."

Astrid bumped Lena with her elbow and shifted her eyes to a woman sitting at one of the sewing machines. Lena didn't see anything of note, but Astrid must have.

"It looks like you found a load of old Victorian treadle machines," she said. "Can we see?"

Marielle smiled in pride. "They were scattered all over old Chicago. We asked people to collect them, and here we are. The belts are leather and don't last very long, but we can replace them."

Lena let the woman get ahead of them and stepped closer to Astrid. "What?"

"She tucked some cloth into her bag," Astrid whispered. "Stealing?"

"We aren't going to turn her in," Lena said. "I don't think we'll be able to talk to her, either."

"Distract Marielle and I'll get what we need."

Lena nodded and stepped forward to ask the woman about a piece of work being done at a machine several feet away.

Two hours later, they were on their way back to the apartment. Lena's saddlebags were filled with notes and fabric samples.

"Okay what did you learn?" she asked Astrid as soon as they were out of earshot of anyone at the warehouse.

"She couldn't talk much," Astrid said, "but I told her we didn't care about what Haven thought. The fabric was for a blanket. Some kids in the orphanages get nothing unless they work."

"Did she actually say orphanages?"

"Yeah. I don't remember seeing places like that around the center."

"No. They're probably here. The fabric trade used kids a lot when it became industrialized. Dangerous work around the looms that adults can't do."

"That's... I don't know, all kinds of wrong, but how else are they going to keep producing?"

Lena couldn't answer the question.

32

Lena and Beattie were assigned work in the communal kitchens the next day. Bread and nutritious stews were made in an old school kitchen and then transported to different areas for distribution. The residents were able to supplement this basic diet with produce bought from the farm shops, and doing their own hunting and fishing. All contributed fifty percent to the community stores, leaving half for their own use or sale. It seemed to work on the surface. No one starved, no one had a free ride.

It was boring to sit through these lectures every time she showed up for a new assignment. But Lena wanted the knowledge, and it was informative to watch people deliver an upbeat version of the history. Like the past was gone and all that mattered was how they got through today and tomorrow. Not a bad philosophy, but nothing was all that positive. Maybe that's why she was convinced Haven held a secret.

Beattie was assigned to the kneading station, and Lena to shaping. Hard work, but it didn't require much expertise.

Lena's baking skills were over a year behind her at the farm. Beattie probably never had the opportunity when she was in training.

"Lena?"

She turned to the sound of her name. Anne was standing at the other end of her table. "I thought you were at the archives," Lena said.

"Took a day off and now I regret it. I was hoping for something outside," Anne said with a laugh. "I got to the job place too late, and this is all I could do. I guess it's a bit better than the libraries. At least here we get to sample the bread and stew fresh. I just got here. You?"

So much for getting away from Anne. Lena reached for the next tray of dough and came up empty. She looked over at Beattie, still kneading.

"Break time," the chef said. "Middle of the line first. Kneaders second, bakers and packers last."

Lena wiped the flour from her hands. It wasn't the fine grind she was used to at home, now that the mills were functioning, but it made a hearty loaf. She followed the other three in her team to a side door. Outside, a picnic table was set up with food and water. The shade was a change from the heat inside and the blast from the direct sun.

Anne sat beside her and passed a serving of food. "Have you been cooking the entire time?"

"This is the first," Lena said, then put a spoonful of stew in her mouth.

"I kind of wish I hadn't taken the archiving job some days," Anne said as she waited for Lena to swallow. "I mean, it's interesting work, but variety is better."

Lena nodded and kept eating. If Anne was digging for information, she wasn't going to get it.

"I heard you visited a couple of the other centers," Anne said. "Did you learn anything useful?"

So, we are being watched.

"Not much. The farmers had a few things Scott found interesting."

Anne broke her bread into chunks and dropped them in the stew. "I don't think the people of Haven are used to answering questions. Did you get any push back?"

"Why would anyone do that? We weren't asking for trade secrets."

Anne poked her spoon into the bowl but didn't eat. "I just think they might not want to share with strangers."

"Is that what the archivists are like?"

"Yes, I guess so. It could be just because we're super busy. Or maybe I'm asking the wrong questions. Da Vinci isn't interested so much in dying cloth or farming."

Like Tik said, the man they'd met on their way west was interested in everything. Improvement at any level was worth the effort. Perhaps things had changed. Maybe he'd had a breakthrough that made the whole of Beta focus on one aspect of making the world easier.

"Not a surprise," Lena said, saving the thought for later discussion, "that they won't give away their secrets. These days, you need an edge. Farming and dying cloth aren't that advanced. People figure out what's best for them. In fact, we might not care how they do the fabric and leather. It could be a trade item for them. It wouldn't be odd to find that different communities are the specialist in things."

Anne started eating, and Lena was left in peace for the time it took for the woman to get through half her lunch. The others had already finished and were chatting at the end of the table. Anne didn't seem hungry. Even though she hadn't done any work yet, she shouldn't be nursing the food like it didn't matter to her.

"How long will you work with the archivist?" Lena asked.

"I don't know," Anne said. "They have a ton of work, so I can probably help through the winter. Alice told me I was doing a good job, so they must be happy for me to stick around."

"I thought Bud was the history guy," Lena said.

Anne took another spoonful of stew and bread. She kept her eyes on the bowl while she chewed. "Alice is doing his history stuff while he's working on some logistics project."

She had to think about her answer.

Was Anne privy to some secret about the city history?

"So, are you going to ask your questions anywhere else?" Anne asked.

"I don't know. The farm isn't like Haven. There are only so many things we can take back."

"Good idea to keep close to home," Anne said. "Have you given any thought to staying here for a season?"

"Break over," the chef called. "Get back to work."

When she set up at the shaping table again, Lena watched as the chef spoke to Anne. Whatever he said, she nodded and left.

The work kept Beattie and Lena separated for the next two hours. No chance to talk about Anne showing up. Or anything else.

The second shift arrived to relieve them, and the chef handed each of the morning team a loaf of bread to take home.

As soon as they arrived in the lobby of their building, Beattie handed her loaf to Lena. "I'm going to check on Scott because he worked alone. I'll grab Strider so I won't be too long getting to the farm."

33

On her way up, Lena stopped on each floor to check for tenants again. She wasn't going to be caught by surprise if things changed.

As Sylvia said, there was one occupied apartment on each floor. Mostly families with children, which made sense to her. Families could take advantage of the younger members' energy and fitness to take the stairs for errands.

The floor below was still empty of people, but someone had left a notice outside the door. If no one was there, as they suspected, then Sylvia was doing a lot of work to pretend they were.

The same notification sat on the floor at their front door. A warning about the storm. So, Anne wasn't a complete pain in the ass. Lena put the notice on the kitchen counter when she got inside. If they stayed, someone would need to plan cooking and other things for when the storm kept them inside. Or they could plan to leave before. A storm on the road wasn't pleasant, but they'd ridden through worse.

She reached for the book she'd been reading last night, and it wasn't there. It was on the coffee table. She remembered dropping it on the couch when she went to bed. No electric light meant no way to safely read in bed.

A glance around made her stomach clench.

Someone had been in their place. Whoever it was had been sloppy. They'd made sure not to leave obvious evidence, but the cushions were in the wrong place. Set up for someone to sink into a corner of the couch. When she'd left that morning, half of them were piled in the middle, pushed there by people who wanted to sit together.

She stifled the streak of curses.

If someone searched, they might be listening. She had no idea how anyone could set up microphones, but spies existed long before technology made it easy.

She'd ask the others to check their bedrooms, but hers looked a little neater than when she and Scott left. The bed was made, but she'd never been one to tuck in the sheets at the foot of the bed.

Time to plan their exit. Storm or not, they weren't safe here.

Lena wrote her observation on a note that she handed to each person as they entered the apartment. Scott and Beattie came last, and Lena tossed the paper in the coals she'd lit to get the grill working. The note read, *someone searched and they might be listening.*

"We should learn some kind of sign language," Astrid muttered as she headed to check the bedroom.

"That storm is coming," Lena said. "Let's talk over dinner."

They needed some kind of background noise to talk on the terrace, but Lena hadn't been able to come up with anything that would last long. Or wouldn't seem purposeful.

"We should try the water feature," Luis said. "It's run on

solar, and I noticed a storage battery, so it should run after sunset. Sylvia probably expects us to test it out."

"They are relaxing for most people," Lena said. "And if the power system works, imagine what else they could use it for."

"Not an elevator," Astrid said. "But yeah, it might cool the air down a bit, too."

Like an old-fashioned air conditioner, Lena thought. Not as effective as a powered one, but easier to use if you had cold water and some way to fan the cooled air around.

They moved to sit around the fountain after cooking the meat Scott brought from the market.

"The storm is coming in a couple of days," Luis said, reading the notice. "Are we leaving before or after? Waiting could mean a week more here."

"Anything missing?" Beattie asked, keeping her voice above a whisper.

No one said anything.

"Why do we have to wait a week?" Astrid asked.

The discussion around the storm was at a normal level. If anyone was listening, they'd get bored.

"If it's as big as they think, there'll be floods," Scott said. "If we want to keep good relationships here, we should stick around to help with clean-up."

"We need to scout more," Beattie said quietly. "I don't want to leave here looking over my shoulder all the way home."

"Do you think we should leave tomorrow, get away from here before it hits?" Luis asked. "I've done both before. Stuck in a community in bad weather, and found a place on the road to wait things out. Both have their downsides."

Lena's preference was to go. And do it close to the time the storm would come through. If whoever was watching them here was busy preparing for floods and other damage, then no one would follow them. And this storm could be coming off the lake. A few hours' ride inland would take them out of the worst of it. But someone was watching them. Anne was hiding something. And Beattie was right. Logical or not, if they left without figuring it out, they might bring trouble home.

34

"What was everyone's day like?" Lena asked. Normal conversation would be a good cover.

"I was in the crèche," Mellow said. "Astrid was upstairs showing teenagers how to care for weapons."

"They were pretty useless," Astrid said. "It's like no one here thinks they need defending."

"I was on stable duty all day, with Luis," Tik said. "Mucking out mostly." He nodded to get Lena's attention on Luis.

He was writing on a scrap of paper handing it to Lena when he finished.

More horses there today. Big ones. Like warhorses. Groom said they were for the plows and wagons. Not sure I believed him.

She passed the message around and then watched as Luis tossed it onto the embers. A tendril of smoke rose as the paper curled in the heat. Luis used a fork to stir the ashes.

"How are the little kids?" Beattie asked. "Haven is lucky they have so many."

"Cute," Mellow said. "It's kind of refreshing to teach kids who aren't scared about the future. These were all born after the plagues died out. Mostly it was playtime and stories. A few little quizzes built into the games. I'm pretty sure it was to check for aptitude. Kind of too young for that, in my opinion. I guess Haven needs to know what skills are in the pipeline though."

"So, you read them Dr. Seuss and played with blocks?" Luis asked. It was like he knew something more was coming.

"They have some new stories," Mellow said. Then she dropped her voice. "One of the kids was a bit too full of energy to settle. Another kid told them the red cloaks would come if they didn't behave. No idea what that is all about."

There were always myths for kids. Some kind of bogeyman to keep them a little scared of acting up. Not all of them were fiction.

"What happened?" she asked. "We might need a good villain to use as more kids are born."

"Everyone settled down. Not just the kid running around. All of them kind of sat up straight and looked like they were trying to be invisible."

35

The next morning, Lena sat with the others in the living room. They'd gone to bed agreeing to think everything through and make the decision over breakfast. With luck, someone had a plan, because Lena didn't.

It was hard to figure out anything without being able to talk to each other. Lena and Scott spent a while quietly offering pros and cons for leaving. The pros were mostly based on their unproven suspicions. The cons on some vague idea the Haven would be a good trading partner. That was if Lena's suspicions were wrong. She acknowledged even if only to herself that it was possible. The betrayals at Pearl Two and Glass House. The trouble at Liberty. All baggage she was using as a barrier against trusting Haven.

Not enough proof either way, and likely wouldn't ever be. If something was wrong here, trying to get proof was dangerous if they were caught. If nothing was wrong, then asking questions could make Haven decide they didn't want anything to do with such suspicious people.

"One more thing," Astrid said. "Proof or otherwise, one more hint things are wrong and we go."

Beattie nodded. "I think it was good we came. Knowledge is better than ignorance."

"We should go now," Luis said. "Do it like there's no big deal. We give Sylvia her report and then we need to get going before the storm. It's a good excuse."

"One more day," Mellow said.

Tik held her hand and then added, "I don't think we visit anyone else. I think we head out tomorrow morning and don't bother to say goodbye. We can leave the stuff for Sylvia here. Seems to me that's going to tell us one way or another. If someone comes after us, there's something wrong. No reason to chase us otherwise."

"We spend today looking for something," Lena said. "I agree, we're out. That storm is due in a couple of days. I can already feel it building. So, what exactly are we going to do?"

"We don't go out alone," Scott said. "That means no one, Tik. If there's something bad happening, we'll see clues around here. Maybe it's happening out in the other centers, but you didn't get much when you visited, right? Only more suspicion and things that could be interpreted both ways."

"The archives," Mellow said. "It's not hard work to sort and catalog books."

"It's too far," Lena said. "And Anne is there. She'll get in the way of any questions."

"I could ask about how they do the sorting," Mellow said, "for our own library. She won't be able to get in the way of that. It's a legitimate question."

"It feels like separating," Lena said.

"Okay, how about we regroup at lunch and decide? It's not that far. We can go in the afternoon and be back before dark. Anne doesn't have any problems traveling back and forth."

If they didn't find anything to support their suspicions or prove there was nothing particularly wrong, Lena would prefer to leave earlier. But she knew herself enough that doing less would haunt her. Before Pearl Two, she would have taken Haven at face value. It was possible that Trixie's actions jaded her, but Lena had given up trusting without proof.

"Scott and I will wander around the stores," she said. "We'll bring lunch to the picnic area near the stables. It'll give us a chance to see those horses."

"Astrid and I can hang out at the school," Mellow said. "Offer ideas about curriculum? Or... we'll think of something."

"That leaves Beattie, Tik and you, Luis," Scott said. "No one goes alone."

"I was thinking we'd ride around the outskirts. See what the lookouts have to say." Luis nodded toward Beattie and Tik. "You'll be handy for talking security."

And then we leave, Lena promised herself. The dread she couldn't quite name kept growing as time passed. She'd tried to convince herself that it was the approaching storm, but it wasn't. Some of it, yes. The changes in pressure could bring on anxiety. But this had been lurking in her mind since leaving the coast. Maybe it wasn't Haven, but just the world right now. Something always seemed to be festering.

"We need to know more about the police," Astrid said. "Maybe you'll see something on your ride, Beattie."

"Take what you don't need for tonight downstairs," Luis said. "That way we won't waste time transferring our belongings in the morning."

Lena and Scott packed their bags when everyone was

gone. "I'm taking it all," she said. "I don't need anything for tonight but a change of clothes. I'll bring that up when we get back."

"I think that's what everyone did," he said. "Let's go. I want to get the most out of the day."

She followed him down the stairs and into the storage locker they'd commandeered. "We might have some debt to clear," she said. "We didn't work much. Should we talk to Sylvia first? Find out if we're in the clear?"

"Hey, maybe they owe us something," Scott said. "We did this stupid test of living on the twentieth floor."

Meeting Sylvia meant they couldn't just sneak out. The risk of leaving debt was too much not to let her know. Haven would have a legitimate claim on them to clear the amount owing. If it couldn't be paid today, then they would leave. The problem was it undercut Tik's idea that someone would only come after them if something was wrong. And without knowing what the police were like, it could be a disaster to get arrested.

"Do it first?" she asked as she looped her arm through his for the stroll. "Gives us a chance to deal with whatever we learn?"

It was a short walk to the welcome center. Sylvia was there talking to Alice, and both women looked up from their conversation when Scott and Lena entered.

"You are looking fit," Alice said. "A bonus of living up there?"

"Hard to be on the road if you're not in shape," Scott said.

Alice excused herself to read some report at a table in the corner. "Running things never lets you have a moment's peace."

Lena told Sylvia they were planning to leave and gave her their impressions of the experiment.

"So maybe it's a flip of before. Young, fit laborers get the prime views?" Sylvia said with a laugh. "Just kidding. We'll rethink the idea until we have some kind of elevator. We have lots of empty apartments on the bottom five floors."

No indication she'd searched the apartment. Sylvia was either a very good actor or not in on the plans. Lena couldn't decide which was more likely.

"You don't owe anything," she said when Scott asked, "but please don't leave right away. There's a picnic and celebration in a couple of days. Fingers crossed the storm will stay away."

"We'll think about it," Lena said, "but you know how long it takes to get anywhere these days."

36

A picnic when a storm warning was just issued? They must have a lot of faith in their predictions. Lena mulled it over as she walked beside Scott. Should they stay? No. Her gut told her it was not a good idea. Even if the party gave them a little more information, the storm would be too close.

"Do you think we should take some of these craft kits?" Scott asked. They'd stopped outside a store that contained fabric, yarn, knitting supplies and other items needed for making homes comfortable.

Lena moved closer to the glass to see the details. "Lots of beginner stuff," she said. "I think we could teach people the basics. Maybe someone in Crystal, or one of the other towns could do more. Even if we keep it simple, it's something to do in the winter. Mittens and scarves for everyone."

"If we can provide the yarn. I was thinking the books," he said, pointing to a shelf on the left of the window display. "How to weave, how to build a loom, others. It would be nice to create our own fabric, even if we don't plan on dying it."

"We are never going to do that," Lena said with a laugh. "I'm not sure I could wear something that I had to smell as it was processed. If no one has done anything about it while we're gone, though, setting up a tannery and some natural way to dye wool would be great. We can't always rely on someone else to do the dirty work."

"There was a bunch of leather goods in Liberty," Scott said. "Not from before, either. Someone is already on the job. Maybe we'll send a delegation in the spring to make a deal."

A commotion behind them caught Lena's attention. Three mounted men in black clothes with red accents were chasing a man down the street. The man didn't try begging for help or running down a side street. There was no way he would escape, and he knew it. Was he trying to distract the riders? So, a partner could get away?

The crowd parted to let the riders get closer to their prey.

A woman standing close to Lena muttered 'thief' under her breath.

"Are those the police?" Lena asked her. Stupid question, but it could prompt more information.

"What we have of them. Peacekeepers. They report to the red cloaks. We don't ask questions."

"I thought they were a story to make kids behave," Scott said, "like a bogeyman."

The riders cut the man off. He tried to slip between the horses, but no one would help him.

A rope swung out over his head, and he was caught in the loop, like a steer at a rodeo.

"What will happen to him?" Lena asked.

"Best you don't know," the woman said and crossed

herself. "Asking the wrong questions can get you in that same noose."

37

W hen they got back to the apartment that afternoon, a note was stuck to the door. Lena opened it before going inside, ready to run if it was a problem.

"Anne's going to meet us for breakfast," she read to Scott. "Say goodbye and give us something to take to Beta."

Scott unlocked the door and put the bag of sandwiches they'd bought on the counter. "I guess we wait for her. At least she'll be here in the morning, so we're not stuck here another day."

Lena lit the grill and placed a kettle on to boil. "After the display this morning, I was hoping to be gone before that."

The crowds had dispersed quickly. When the sidewalk cleared, Scott and Lena walked for a few blocks around the craft store. When nothing else grabbed their attention, they'd traded a few of their goods for handwritten and drawn copies of ten how-to books. Those were stuffed into a bag in the locker.

By the time tea was ready, Astrid arrived with a crate of

sodas. "Mellow is on her way. I got these from that Alice woman. A treat, she said."

"What does she do around here?" Lena asked. "I don't remember. She was reading reports this morning, but I didn't ask what they were."

"Didn't Anne say she was covering for that Bud guy?" Astrid asked. She pried off one of the caps and took a gulp. "Still too sweet, and I don't like the bubbles."

Lena was glad the girl wouldn't get a taste for something so unhealthy.

"Did anyone see Tik, Beattie, or Luis?" Astrid asked. "I don't want to go over what we all found more than once. We need all the information to make a final decision."

"We should eat now," Lena said. "Save enough for everyone and some breakfast." She tossed Anne's note on the counter. "We'll have a guest."

Astrid read the note and rolled her eyes. "Please don't let her join us."

Lena grinned at Astrid's teenage reaction.

Scott walked out to the terrace and looked over the side. Eating could wait a little, it was only just after two. "Let's hope she doesn't make us feel obligated."

"They're here," Scott called. "Just rode into the garage."

Between settling the horses and making the trek up to the apartment, it was twenty minutes before the three companions walked through the door. In the time they waited, everyone showered and did a final check of their belongings. Regardless of what secret Haven hid, a warm shower was a luxury.

Another bag of food came with them, and a crate of beer. "Everyone is very generous," Tik said. "Just be careful not to get a hangover."

Lena sorted through the food and put aside bread and butter for the morning. The rest would be shared between the group, with any leftovers going into their saddlebags tomorrow.

"The lookouts are probably the least informed citizens of Haven," Beattie said. "They get sent out on ten-day shifts in pairs. They have a line of sight to the other teams. No one knew about the storm, or basically anything."

"We didn't see any police," Tik said. "I guess if we'd done this earlier, some of us could have gone all around the city. Maybe they don't have to work hard. People are so happy to be safe and kept in food and shelter they don't commit crimes."

Lena shook her head at Scott. Their story should come last.

"The school was all getting ready for the pre-harvest party," Mellow said. "Apparently, people are too busy after harvest to do much celebrating."

The conversation slowed down as everyone ate. When the packaging was in the waste bins and everyone had a beer, Lena explained what she and Scott witnessed.

"Holy shit," Astrid said. "And everyone just watched?"

"Not just that," Scott said. "They were scared. The woman who spoke to us didn't take her eyes off the cops."

"And they just dragged him off?" Beattie asked.

"Not dragged. The horses were slow enough for him to keep his feet," Lena said.

"I guess if he stole something, it makes sense they chased him," Luis said. "I'm more concerned about the crowd. If the cops don't get any resistance, or create that kind of terror, the punishment must be harsh; chopping off hands, hanging."

"So, the red cloaks are real," Mellow said. "Not great, right?"

"It might be nothing," Lena said. "People would scare their kids with the cops as much as they did a bogeyman. But we should go as soon as Anne leaves tomorrow morning. I don't want to know anything else about how they keep the peace here."

38

T he next morning, everyone was up at sunrise. Waiting for Anne to arrive frustrated Lena more than she expected. Breakfast wasn't a leisurely event anywhere these days. People's shifts started a couple of hours after sunrise, and most were required to commute.

"How long do we give her?" Tik asked.

Lena checked her watch: nine thirty. "I don't want to just leave. If she has something for Da Vinci, we should take it."

"Do we go looking for her?" Astrid asked. "To the archives, I mean. Not all of Haven."

"Give her more time," Beattie said. "Imagine the fun you'll have yelling at her for holding us up."

Two hours later, Anne still hadn't turned up.

"I can't just leave her," Lena said. "What if we get packed and a couple of us ride out to the archives? See if we can track her down for whatever she wants us to take to Beta."

"I don't like the idea," Tik said. "Not trying to find her, yeah, I get that we'd worry. And how would we explain it to

Da Vinci? But I say one of us goes. The rest pack and head out to a place we can meet up."

"That way we'll be out of the city," Astrid said. "I like it. I'll go."

"It can't be you," Beattie said. "You don't like her, and she knows it. Whoever heads out takes their horse and that's it. Everything else will come with the group."

It wasn't much of a plan, and only three people could reasonably go. Tik, Beattie, or Astrid. Beattie was right. Anne was more likely to get her back up than cooperate with Astrid.

"I think it would be better for two people to go," she said, "but one can move faster. Fine. Decide who's going, but we're not leaving Haven without everyone. So come back here. We'll wait in the stables."

"Tik," Beattie said. "He's able to handle himself. Astrid and I will get everyone ready. And no one is going to mess with us if two soldiers are in the group."

THE TRIP to the archives and back was only about forty minutes. Lena thought Anne might be hard to find since something kept her from breakfast. When Tik hadn't returned three hours later, they all stopped pretending nothing was wrong.

"We have to go after him," Mellow said. "If we take all of our stuff, we can just head out of Haven from somewhere around the archives."

"I don't think it makes sense for us to take everything we own into jeopardy," Luis said, "but we need to get closer. When we find out what happened, there's no point coming all the way back. And if it's bad, then we don't want to bring it back here, where there are so many people."

"There's an old mall near the archives," Astrid said. "What? I rode around a lot. Weapons maintenance classes were only a few hours. Lots of free time."

"We go to the mall," Scott said. "From there, we figure out what to do. Is there a decent way out of Haven near the mall?"

"Not the way we came in," Beattie said. "Did you think I was going to let Astrid scout by herself? We'd be heading out more along the shore. But there are places we can shelter along the way."

"So, I'm the idiot," Lena said. "Did anyone else wander around?"

"Not me," Luis said. "I had enough on my hands with keeping an eye on the people around us."

"I didn't get jobs that gave me time," Scott said. "The plan is good, Lena. And you know once we get past the center, we can ride faster. We go to the mall. We decide what to do."

"Okay," she said. "Tik is going to be pissed if we ride in to rescue him when he doesn't need it, but I don't care."

"He's going to be more pissed if he actually needs rescuing," Mellow said.

39

The mall was dirty and showed some evidence of the rioting that happened everywhere as the body count rose. In here, storefronts were a heap of tempered glass cubes, spiderwebs festooned the atrium and the contents of stores were strewn about. Wasted for anyone who survived the plagues and the early violence.

"I guess there isn't a reason to clean it up, yet," Astrid said. "It would make a great market if they did. Indoors, places for people to socialize, stores instead of stalls. Maybe Liberty should look at these places."

Lena turned away as a flood of regret filled her. She closed her eyes and saw the mall in the old days, full of teenagers hanging out, shoppers, and seniors looking for exercise.

"The parking lots could be converted to stables," Luis said. "Hard work to remove the surface, but not impossible."

"Stop it," Mellow shouted. "Tik has been gone too long. This chatter isn't getting him rescued."

They'd arrived at the mall only a few minutes ago. Instead of planning a rescue, they'd fallen into reminiscing or looking for future uses. Mellow was right. They should have decided on a plan by now. Not just decided on one, they should have been on the road to rescue Tik.

"Okay, Astrid and Beattie should go," Lena said. "We'll keep close to the entrance so you don't have to come find us."

"I can set up watch in the parking lot," Luis said. "In one of the abandoned cars. Just in case we need to move faster."

"I'm going with them," Mellow said. "If anyone is hurt, they'll need me."

"We'll be faster and sneaker by ourselves," Astrid said.

"I am coming." Mellow mounted River and glared at the two soldiers when they didn't immediately move.

"Drop the saddlebags," Astrid said. "Do everything we tell you. Do you have weapons?"

Mellow undid the strap of one of the two bags and let it drop. "Knives. And this other bag has medical supplies."

"Be careful," Lena said, "and be quick. We can camp here overnight, but I'd rather be on our way even if it's late."

40

Lena was stroking Bebop's neck in an effort to keep herself calm. The archives were only ten minutes away from the mall. Far enough these days to be safe if no one came looking.

Getting there and scouting for a vantage point, maybe ten more minutes. If they needed to rescue Tik, or Anne... she stopped trying to estimate times. It had been an hour. If they didn't return, it made no sense to send another rescue party.

To get her people back, Lena was prepared to attack the archives. But it would be a blind assault. "We should have come to see this place," she said. "Visited, even if Anne was there."

"No real reason to," Scott said. "Don't second guess."

"We wrote off Anne," Lena said. "If we thought of her as one of the team, we would have checked."

"She did her best to alienate us," Scott said. "And she was fine when she visited. What makes you think we would have seen something wrong?"

At least he isn't pretending it's all a misunderstanding.

"If no one comes back to report in the next half hour, we're dropping the supplies and going in with bows loaded."

Luis pulled open the door and hissed. "Mellow is coming. It doesn't look good."

If it was just Mellow, it was a problem.

Luis kept the door open to let her ride through. Then he let it slam closed. Mellow was riding low in the saddle. Blood covered her clothes and crusted on her face.

"Where are you hurt?" Lena grabbed the medical supplies bag from Mellow's saddle.

"It's not me," she whispered.

Luis handed her a waterskin and a wet cloth. "Clean your face, drink, then tell us."

She pressed her lips together as if ready to argue and then nodded. The cloth removed some of the blood, but not all. She tossed it into a corner and drained the waterskin.

"They have Tik. The red cloaks. I don't know why they are torturing him. We saw him tied up to the wall. He's been beaten. You need to run now. Astrid and Beattie are fighting."

"Whose blood?" Scott asked.

"A red cloak. Astrid just took his head off. She was so mad, I don't know if she knew what she was doing."

"We're going to help," Lena said. "Were you followed?"

"They didn't know I was there. Beattie made a distraction so I could get away. The blood hit me just before I left."

"Tell us everything," Luis said. "You'll stay here with the pack horses. Hide, in case someone comes looking. We'll go help bust Tik out."

"I'm not leaving him. And Beattie said you should run."

"We're not going to do that," Scott said. "If we're not back by dark, you take everything on the road. We'll find you."

"I can't leave Tik," Mellow said.

"You aren't leaving him," Lena said. "Are you able to kill these red cloaks? We are, and someone needs to protect our backs."

Mellow bit her lip and looked around at the faces. "No. You are right. Tik needs people who won't hesitate to do what's needed. They're in a brick building toward the back of the complex. We only saw ten or so of them near the doors. We found the stables, and Storm is there. Astrid and Beattie left Raven and Strider with the herd. No one was tending them."

"Did you recognize anyone?" Luis asked.

"That Alice woman was in the room with Tik. A man I've never seen was with them. Another woman was there, but we couldn't see her more than a shadow."

Three red cloaks and whoever was left of the ones at the door against determined attack. It was possible if many more people had not come to the aid of the assholes. Lena mounted Bebop. "We do the same. But we'll pull the horses together so we can get out fast. Mellow, we'll be back before nightfall for sure. I'm hoping we don't have unwanted company. Be ready."

Mellow nodded and then turned away.

41

The paddock was still untended, and it took only a few moments to gather all their horses in one area and tether them in a group. The other animals were getting nervous because of the sounds of a battle nearby. They weren't trained for fighting, so they crowded the far fencing. Their own horses were trained enough to stay calm.

"At least we don't have to go find the fight," Scott said. "That must be where they're keeping Tik." He nodded toward a square brick building.

"Maybe he's not the only one," Luis said. "We going to free everyone?"

"Only if it doesn't threaten our escape," Lena said. "These people knew what they agreed to when they set this up."

"Bows ready," Scott said. "I'm guessing Astrid and Beattie are just down that alley."

"I'm going to the building," Luis said. "If you keep the red cloaks busy, I'll get Tik free."

He was gone before Lena or Scott could change his mind.

"It's the best plan," Scott told her. "He'll find a way to tell us he's done. Our job is to keep the assholes distracted."

Lena nodded and slipped ahead of him into the alley. The fight was on the steps of the brick building. A library in the old days, by the signage. The big wooden doors made it easier for the defenders, but someone was making them come through and fight.

Beattie was taking on two people with a sword while Astrid used her crossbow. Bodies lay on the steps as evidence of their success. Far more than the ten Mellow reported.

A man ran out through the doors screaming a battle cry only to receive a bolt through his neck. Beattie stumbled, but Lena raised her bow and shot the man standing over her. Neither woman turned to see who'd joined their side.

Scott slipped out of the alley to help Beattie while Lena took cover in a doorway. The stairs might be wide, but adding another fighter at the front was more likely to be a detriment.

The door swung open to let another fighter out, this one in full red cloak uniform. A woolen short cape dyed blood red, over crimson shirt and pants. The cape hood was drawn down enough to obscure the face from the nose up. The fighter pulled a disc from the bag hanging from their belt.

Astrid thrust her sword through her last opponent's neck, her empty crossbow on the ground. She swore and grabbed for pouch at her hip when she saw the new figure.

The red cloak smiled and turned to throw her weapon at Beattie. Lena knew that smile. A little snide and turned down on one side. Anne.

Astrid spun her own metal star to meet Anne's. Like some kind of martial arts movie, the two throwing stars clashed in mid-flight. Lena didn't have time to admire the skill. She aimed carefully and released her bolt, missing Astrid's shoulder by a hair and sinking into Anne's red cloaked chest.

No other soldiers came through the door.

Lena hurried to join the others on the steps.

"We have to rush it," Astrid said. "I don't think there are many inside."

She ran to the door and hurled her body at it. The door swung wide, and Beattie slipped in, running to the right. Astrid rolled from the force and then leaped to her feet, running to the left.

"You go with Beattie," Scott said as he crept through the gap.

Inside, the place was deserted. Beattie and Astrid had already completed a search to make sure no one was hiding behind one of the low shelves in the main part of the room.

"We saw Tik through a window," Astrid gasped out. "Down that corridor. On the left."

42

When they reached the door, Lena stood to the side as Beattie kicked it in and then dropped to avoid any weapon coming her way. No resistance.

They raced in to see Tik tied to a wall, blood dripping from cuts on his chest.

"Drop your weapons," a familiar voice ordered.

Alice stood in the corner with Luis on his knees before her. His arm was twisted up to hold him in place. A knife at his throat.

"Do as she says," Lena told the others. Then, turning to Alice, she tried to get control of the situation. "Let him go."

"I cannot," Alice said. "You are all a danger to Haven. He will die first, and then the rest of you will follow one by one. My soldiers will take you to cells to wait. A place where you'll hear the screams of your friends."

Did she have a fresh supply of soldiers? Lena doubted it. Any fighter who hid while his or her teammates were slaughtered was probably well on their way out of the city.

"Let them go," Astrid said. "We're leaving now. You won't have to worry about us."

"Perhaps if you had done so on the day you arrived, then you would have been safe. You know too much."

Luis turned his head to look up at Lena. "She's not kidding." He flashed a glance toward Astrid.

"No one is coming to the rescue," Lena said. "Just let us go. We don't care what happens here."

Alice glanced to the door. "Anne said you were good, but no one can kill that many soldiers without getting hurt. You are weakened and out of bolts."

"Your guys never had to fight for their lives, right?" Beattie asked. "Training and actually killing an enemy are two very different things. They fought like there were rules."

"You still won't get out," Alice said. "I know you won't leave these two. And I'm not letting them go. Anne reported on your loyalty to each other as she led you here."

Something flew past Lena's ear and embedded itself into Alice's throat. A throwing star.

Luis pulled to the side as the woman slumped. He rolled away from her body and groaned as he stood. "What a freak. Are they all dead?"

Beattie and Astrid untied Tik while Scott and Lena helped Luis.

"We don't know if there are others," Scott said. "I'd guess by the number of horses, we dealt with everyone who was here. Reinforcements? If we can get out of here fast, they are Haven's problem."

"Haven knows this whole thing is here," Tik said. "I don't know how much, but some are aware of this torture business."

"Take them to the horses and get ready. Mellow can look

over Tik," Lena said. "Scott and I are going to have a quick look around. Maybe find answers."

"I'll come with you," Luis said. "I'm not hurt, just sore. I might recognize details you don't."

There really wasn't time to argue, so Lena nodded at Astrid. "Go make sure we're ready to run as soon as we join you."

"You have fifteen minutes," Beattie said. "We're coming for you after that."

Lena and Scott broke through each door on the first floor, hoping to find an office. The second and third floors would take too much time to search.

The office was on the opposite side of the library from the cell where Alice held Tik. The door gave no resistance to a shove, but everything inside was locked.

"Be quick," Lena said. "We've got seven minutes before rescue arrives. So just smash locks or whatever."

"This," Luis said, holding up a ledger. "List of names. We got the bulk of their forces. The peacekeepers don't seem to be part of it. It looks like Alice was picking assholes for the job, rather than bringing them into the inner circle."

"Then we'll be safe," Scott said. "What we saw of Haven tells me they aren't all in on it."

Lena checked her watch. "We have to go."

They ran to the front doors. Scott looked through in case there were threats waiting. "It's clear."

"Heretics!"

Lena turned, raising her cross bow.

A man stood behind the desk at the front.

Luis stepped forward, his arms raised in a calming pose.

The man picked up a knife and raised it to throw.

Lena shot.

The man collapsed.

Luis grunted and fell to his knees.

43

Scott dragged Lena away from where she knelt at Luis's body. "He's gone. We can't do anything for him."

Lena blinked and nodded but she couldn't move. Scott's voice was choked with the same emotion she felt. Not just the loss of a companion, but the end of her dreams of Luis at the farm.

"We'll talk about him tonight," Scott said. He cleared his throat before continuing. "Don't let his death be for nothing."

This time she placed a kiss on Luis's forehead and said, "Astrid will have a Viking ceremony we can use. You rest now."

She allowed Scott to pull her up and lead her away from the carnage. By the time they approached the paddock, Astrid and Beattie were already making preparations to search for them.

"Luis?" Astrid asked. "How long do we have to wait for him?"

Tears pooled in Lena's eyes and her throat tightened. She shook her head and took Bebop's reins. "Let's go."

They rode in silence until they reached a strip mall just before dark, far enough from Haven they could relax a little. Tik was almost asleep from his ordeal. Scott was riding with him on Beauty; the horse was tiring fast with the weight of two men on his back.

"The outdoors store," Beattie said after scouting the entire area. "Cleaned out by someone who was careful. Room for the horses, and there's water somewhere because those trees look healthy."

They settled for the night in the center of the REI, with the horses toward the back. The scavengers had been more than careful. The shelves were empty but not turned over. Someone had laid artificial turf on the floor, but no one had been in residence for a long time.

"We need a wake," Astrid said, "but we don't have any alcohol."

"Even if we did, getting blasted this close to enemy territory is worse than stupid." Beattie dug into the sacks of food supplies. "We can rearrange everything and use Junior as a pack."

"What would the Vikings do?" Tik asked. He was lying on a pile of their sleeping bags. His wounds were superficial, but so many that all his energy went to healing.

"We need the body, and I'm pretty sure setting a bonfire to burn his trinkets is almost as bad as getting drunk." Astrid joined Beattie.

"We have honey and tea and some fresh food," Beattie said. "There's enough Sterno left to keep a camp stove going. I don't care what traditions were before. Tonight, we make our own. We talk about him, and cry and whatever we need to do."

"I'll set up some alarms," Scott said. "Just a warning if someone tries to get in."

Mellow sat beside Tik, fussing over his wounds and whispering. Lena, still numb from losing Luis, started the stove and dug out cups.

"Why?" she asked. "Did they say why they took you, Tik?"

He looked up from his conversation with Mellow. "Some religious crap. They were the same as that Ambrose guy. We were asking too many questions. Maybe we were scouting for an attack by heathens? It was all weird."

He pushed himself off the bedding and moved closer to the stove. Mellow dragged the sleeping bags around the camp so they could all have a cushion between them and the concrete floor. "I mean it, Tik. No exertion. Let the balm work."

"Talking around the fire isn't doing me harm," he said. "We should probably wait until Scott gets back before starting. Anne was part of it from the beginning. I did learn that. The whole story about Beta was bullshit. I get the feeling Ambrose sent her to get us. I'm pretty sure the religious stuff was a cover-up for revenge."

"The soldiers we killed," Lena said. "How would they know?"

The door opened and everyone reached for weapons. Scott. He was holding empty bottles and cans. "Relax, it's me. I'll pile these up to trip anyone sneaking in."

When the tea and food were ready, no one seemed prepared to start talking about Luis. Lena couldn't find the words either, so she asked Tik to tell them all the details.

"There's not much more. They asked about home, but I wouldn't tell them anything — at least we were smart enough to keep that from Anne. Alice lost interest and started with the heretic and heathen stuff."

"I still come back to how they knew about the soldiers we killed," Mellow said. "We made sure there weren't any hanging around after the fight. When that last one killed himself, who would have told?"

"Maybe you missed someone?" Astrid said. "If I was observing and saw you kill all my unit, I'd get out to make the report before you could come looking."

"Or the guy lied," Tik said, "when he said Ambrose was too far away to care. Maybe they were a day or two behind and figured it out when they found the bodies."

"There's another explanation," Beattie said. "Don't assume the wandering monks knew what was going on. Anne might have been with those soldiers, making sure Ambrose was keeping on track. She decided on her own to come after us for, I don't know, revenge maybe."

"We did feel like someone was following us a lot," Mellow said. "You found the cougar and that girl from Crouch, but maybe Anne was there too."

"When she knew we were headed for Liberty, she could have beaten us there," Astrid said. "The time we spent side-tracking to Nation One. That's how long she was in the market."

"We'll never know," Lena said. "And since they're all learning if heaven and hell actually exist now, we need to let it go."

"Remember when we first met Luis," Mellow said, "and you, Astrid, how you got him in trouble?"

Astrid grimaced at the memory. "You know that was the only weapon I had as Jane. But he never tried anything. In Virtue, he could have done whatever he wanted to me as long as he married me."

"He was honorable," Tik said, "and maybe you reminded him of his own kids."

"That dinner the night we left Pearl Two," Lena said. "He was so excited to spoil us."

44

No one tripped the alarm overnight.

The reminiscing had lasted until first Tik and then Astrid dropped off to sleep, followed closely by Beattie and Mellow. Scott and Lena sat guard until dawn, both too wound up to rest.

As the sun rose, Scott woke everyone while Lena prepared breakfast.

She felt less numb as she lit the last of the Sterno to make tea. Luis's absence was like a wound. She counted the mugs and realized she'd put one out for him. She blinked away tears and told herself grief needed to wait. They were still too close to Haven to relax.

Perhaps at the farm they could put a headstone for him. Even though no one there would know who he was, his story could continue.

The door opened.

Lena reached for her weapon, but it was across the camp stove from her. How could she have been so careless?

Astrid and Beattie were already on their feet with swords

in hand. Scott stood beside Tik, both had bows drawn. Mellow held a knife ready to defend the group.

"Peace," Frank, the city planner from Haven, said. "We're not here to fight."

Behind him, three strangers stood with Sylvia. All had their hands up to the side. Away from the weapons they carried, but still able to reach them in the event of a fight.

"Why did you follow us?" Lena said. She stood to the side so she wouldn't hinder any defense.

"To thank you," Frank said. "It was you, right? Your friend's body was there, so..."

"You mean the red cloaks?" Astrid said. "The people you let kidnap Tik and torture him? The people who enforced your laws with brutality? Your city is a lie."

"I know it looks that way but give us a moment to explain. Those people held us hostage," Sylvia said. "We were struggling when they arrived from the west. They said they'd been kicked out of a community in the mountains. When they first set up, they helped us. The Church of the Pure. Seemed like a godsend."

The cult Greeley kicked out of Fort Redemption? Lena looked at Beattie, who nodded.

"And when did they turn you into idiots?" Astrid said. "Why do you think they were kicked out?"

"This would be easier if we could relax," Frank said. "At least can we put down our arms?"

"Drop your weapons, then we can talk."

Swords and bows hit the floor, bolts joined them, and Sylvia added a handful of throwing knives. When they were done, Astrid searched them to confirm nothing was hidden.

"Okay, join us for tea," Mellow said. "I'm not sure how you can convince us that a small group of people could take over a whole community."

The story didn't take long. The Church of the Pure gained followers through results. Haven would have dissolved like so many other communities without their help. Their power grew until suddenly they controlled everything. Still only a core of people, but peaceful lives and sufficient food went a long way to buying loyalty.

"There are maybe fifty people out there trying to convert others," Sylvia said. "When you came with Anne, we assumed you were part of a plan. So, we let you do what you wanted, we gave you the apartment. There was no experiment, Lena. Who would want to live like that?"

"What you did cut off the head," Frank said. "We have our community back and we intend to live up to the name of Haven. It'll take us some time to get trust back and root out the remnants of their followers. I guess we've found a belief system that we can't tolerate."

"And the ones on the road?" Lena asked. "They aren't just trying to convert people. We ran into them and their soldiers."

"Like I said, there are only a few groups," Sylvia said. "They report back periodically. We've noticed they have a high attrition rate; seems like they aren't all that prepared for life on the road even with armed escorts. We'll handle them as they come back — probably soon, to avoid the hardship of winter on the road. Maybe in the spring we can send out our own scouts to deal with the remnants."

"Kill them?" Astrid asked.

"If they fight, we will not hold back," Frank said, "but we don't plan on destroying them."

"We're leaving," Lena said. "Thank you for telling us this. We can warn people about the monks on our way home."

"Your friend," Frank said. "He will be a hero. We won't let his death go unnoticed. I am deeply sorry for your loss."

Luis the hero? Lena smiled. She wasn't sure how he'd feel about it, but she liked the idea of him being honored.

"Good luck on your journey," Sylvia said. "We brought a few bags of supplies for you. They're outside."

When the sound of the visitors' horses faded, Scott and Beattie retrieved the gifts.

"More Sterno," Astrid said. "That means fewer nights trying to find fuel for a fire."

"Cloth," Mellow said, "and books, handbound. How to build the new improvements they've developed for everything." She flipped some pages. "This is huge. Maybe we can make copies? Lots of people will trade for these, right?"

Not the lightest supplies, Lena thought. Knowledge was worth the trouble, though, and maybe this was the way to unite people. Sharing methods to make life easier.

45

The journey to Beta was uneventful. Their path took them through Milwaukee and Duluth, along with a handful of tiny farming communities. Both large towns were inhabited, but unlike Haven, they traded with each other and the smaller settlements. The best part, as far as Lena was concerned, none of the places gave anyone a twinge of suspicion that something was wrong under the veneer.

They shared the knowledge from Haven, staying long enough for someone to duplicate the contents of the books. In Duluth, a handful of the monks were in jail and the local sheriff was grateful for the information Lena shared. The prisoners were prepared for transport to Haven the next morning.

THEY ARRIVED at Beta mid-morning after discussing the remainder of their trip. Two days' hard ride from home, rather than the weeks they took exploring more than a year ago.

"It looks the same," Scott said. "The gate is stronger, but I don't see any reason for it."

"No dead bodies," Astrid said. "What's that awful noise?"

"Machinery working," Tik said.

No one came out to see what six strangers wanted, but Lena had no illusions that Beta didn't know they were waiting to enter.

"If we hang out here too long, we'll waste the day," Mellow said. "I want to get home. This visit needs to be fast. If Anne did come from here, then all our assumptions are wrong. And Alice lied, and Haven is still a problem."

Does that matter? If Anne was on a mission from Da Vinci, Lena wasn't sure there was anything they could or needed to do about it.

"Fine," she said. "Follow me and be nice, Astrid."

"I'm always nice," Astrid muttered as she fell in line behind Scott.

The guard at the gate welcomed them in. "You've been here before," he said. "You know where the hall is, right?"

Lena nodded and led the group to the stables, and then the armory to store their weapons and belongings. "Is Da Vinci around?" she asked the armorer.

"Go talk to Alfred," the woman said. "We don't have time for gossip around here."

In the hall, only a few people sat at tables eating or drinking. This was the dining hall, the meeting place, and the official building for Beta. Lena didn't recognize any faces. But that didn't mean anything, she told herself.

"Hi," a man called from the far end of the room as he stood and waved. He was with two women who remained sitting. "You must be Lena, right?"

When they were sitting around the long cafeteria table

with iced tea and bread, Alfred asked, "You've been on the road all this time?"

"It's a big journey," she said. "Is Da Vinci coming back soon?"

He looked at his companions as if waiting for them to speak. "He's gone. Went on a scavenging run, told him he should stick close. The team said he just didn't come back one night. Looked for him, no signs."

"Lots of bandits out there," Beattie said. "You in charge now?"

"We don't have much trouble with those kinds of travelers," the blond woman said. "Name's Julie. It would be just like Da Vinci to get himself in trouble looking for a bit of pipe. Or fall off a cliff. We run Beta now. Me, Alfred, and Zia here."

Or he'd run into some monks, Lena thought. "We've got some books," Lena said. "From a community in old Chicago. They've made a lot of discoveries. I can give you a copy we had made."

"Always looking for new ideas," Alfred said. "News, too."

"We have that," Scott said. "Do you have time now? We'd like to get on the road before it's too late to go far."

"You can stay in the barracks overnight if you like," Zia said. "The roads are safe, but not well maintained. Had a few bad storms last winter, more holes than surface in some places. Leave tomorrow. Share your stories at dinner?"

Beattie and Astrid would want to see the armory and figure out what they could trade to get the best product. Lena didn't want to deny them the treat. "A night in the barracks sounds good. You might not want all our stories shared directly with everyone."

"Then give us the highlights," Julie said. "We can decide

what to share. And you can tell us the details of anything we might want to keep secret."

Scott took Astrid and Beattie on a tour. Tik and Mellow went to the farms and medical center, leaving Lena to tell the story of their travels.

She told them about the dangers they'd encountered, the people they should be on the lookout for.

"Oh. Da Vinci would have gotten on the wrong side of the monks," Alfred said. "I'm sure you have lots of good stories, but I agree, we need to filter the bad news."

"You know," Zia said, "you didn't just travel from place to place, right? Some of the communities you visited now have the chance to be better. And you shared so much that will level the playing field between large and small communities."

Lena smiled, but she'd have to think more about their last year to agree with Zia.

"We might think of sending some scouts to a few places next year," Julie said. "This Haven sounds like a great place to do research if they stick on the right path."

"Liberty might be better as your first mission," Lena said. "You might even be able to outsource your scavenging."

"It would be nice to just focus on our inventions," Zia said.

"So, you haven't sent anyone out before?" Lena didn't want to ask outright if Anne came from Beta. Too easy for them to lie that way.

"Da Vinci was talking about it since you left," Julie said, "but we haven't prioritized it yet. From what you say, maybe that was a bad idea. Not knowing is dangerous. And most travelers aren't good at sharing."

46

The residents of Beta were grateful for the news, even if there were giant holes in what Alfred and company agreed to share. The night in the barracks was restful, and the offer of laundry services was unexpected. Lena hoped it wasn't because of how badly they smelled.

Zia's assessment of the road conditions was a slight exaggeration. The horses managed the broken surface well at a walk. Now that everyone traveled by foot or on horse, the roads were simply a convenient way to save time. Lena hoped it wouldn't be long before trade grew, and someone would repair the worst of the damage to allow carts and wagons to move from community to settlement.

"Tomorrow." Mellow rode beside Lena, interrupting her thoughts.

"Really early?" Lena asked. "We could get moving pre-dawn. Just enough light to be safe. We'd be there for lunch."

"I like that idea," Mellow said. "Tomorrow night in our own beds? Heaven. Maybe we can sleep in."

If nothing goes wrong, or if the farm is still safe.

Lena hated that voice in her head. Yes, it was a survival tool on the road, but she didn't want to think something would stop them this close to home.

Of course, she'd thought Luis was safe right up until he died.

"IT LOOKS THE SAME," Scott said. "Well, the new building aside. The farmhouse is still standing, and the barn."

No one came out to see who rode up. Lena couldn't decide if that was a good or bad sign.

"Everyone will be at harvest," Tik said. "We have to go in, Lena."

One more minute of everything being right with the world. Lena took a deep breath and closed her eyes. Remembering how close they'd been to dying on the road to the farm six years ago. And protecting it from strangers who wanted to take it.

She could smell baking bread. Someone was in the kitchen.

In the distance, shouts as people gathered the crops. A dog barked. A baby cried.

"Lena? Are you going to sit on that horse all day?" Ava asked.

Lena opened her eyes to see her friend standing on the porch, a baby cradled in her arms.

FREE BOOK

Claim your copy of Running The Game when you sign up for my newsletter and cheer on Pen as she vies for a commission in the military aboard ship. In the Humanity Found space opera series

ALSO BY P A WILSON

For more books by P A Wilson

Use the QR code below or go to pawilson.ca

ABOUT P A WILSON

Perry Wilson is a Canadian author based in Vancouver, BC who has big ideas and an itch to tell stories. Having spent some time on university, a career, and life in general, she returned to writing in 2008 and hasn't looked back since (well, maybe a little, but only while parallel parking).

She is a member of the Vancouver Writers Social Group, The Royal City Literary Arts Society, and The Surrey Writing Workshop. Perry has self-published several novels. She writes the Madeline Journeys, a fantasy series about a high-powered lawyer who finds herself trapped in a magical world, the Quinn Larson Quests, which follows the adventures of a wizard named Quinn who must contend with volatile fae in the heart of Vancouver, and the Charity Deacon Investigations, a mystery thriller series about a private eye who tends to fall into serious trouble with her cases, and The Riverton Romances, a series based in a small town in Oregon, one of her favorite states. Her stand-alone novels are Breaking the Bonds, Closing the Circle, and The Dragon at The Edge of The Map.

For more information
www.pawilson.ca
pawilson@pawilson.ca

ACKNOWLEDGMENTS

People think that the process of writing is solitary. That's not the case for me. I have help from so many people it would be hard to acknowledge everyone, but I'll give it a try.

The support and inspiration I get from my writer's groups is incalculable. The Vancouver Writers Social Group opens my mind to other ways of telling a story. The Royal City Literary Arts Society gives me the opportunity to meet and share with other writers who have more knowledge than I do. The Other 11 Months group is where I learn about getting the words on the page. And my critique group who helps me find the best parts of the story I want to tell. Thanks to all of the members of these great groups.

Last of all, but definitely a huge part of the process, my beta readers. These are the people who love stories and are willing, and more than able, to tell me if my finished story is ready for you, my readers.